THE
ONLY
PROBLEM

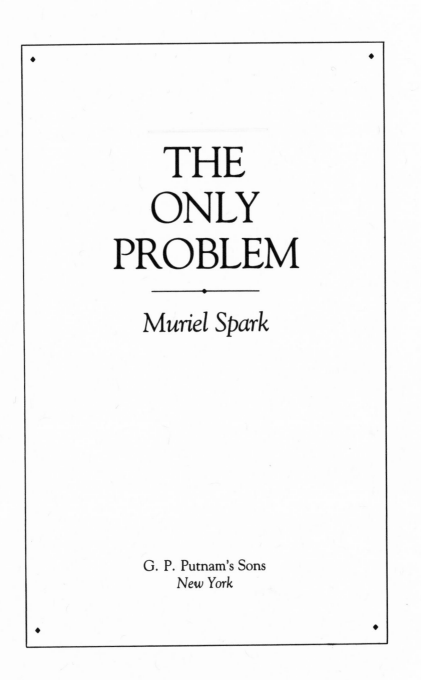

THE
ONLY
PROBLEM

Muriel Spark

G. P. Putnam's Sons
New York

A signed first edition of this book has been
privately printed by The Franklin Library.

Library of Congress Cataloging in Publication Data

Spark, Muriel.
The only problem.

I. Title.
PR6037.P2905   1984   823'.914   83-26203
ISBN 0-399-12987-1

Printed in the United States of America

*Surely I would speak to the Almighty,
and I desire to reason with God.*

—the Book of Job, 13:3

PART I

I

He was driving along the road in France from St. Dié to Nancy in the district of Meurthe; it was straight and almost white, through thick woods of fir and birch. He came to the grass track on the right that he was looking for. It wasn't what he had expected. Nothing ever is, he thought. Not that Edward Jansen could now recall exactly what he had expected; he tried, but the image he had formed faded before the reality like a dream on waking. He pulled off at the track, forked left and stopped. He would have found it interesting to remember exactly how he had imagined the little house before he saw it, but that, too, had gone.

He sat in the car and looked for a while at an old green garden fence and a closed gate, leading to a piece of overgrown garden. There was no longer a visible path to the stone house, which was something like a lodge-keeper's cottage with loose tiles and dark, neglected windows. Two shacks of crumbling wood stood apart from the house. A wider path, on Edward's side of the gate, presumably led to the château where he had no present interest. But he noticed that the car-tracks on the path were overgrown, very infrequently used, and yet the grass that spread over that path was greener than on the ground before him, inside the gate. If his wife had been there he would have pointed this out to her as a feature of Harvey Gotham, the man he had come to see; for he had a theory, too unsubstantiated to be formulated in public, but which he could share with Ruth, that people have an effect on the natural greenery around them regardless of whether they lay hands on it or not; some people, he would remark, induce fertility in their environment and some the desert, simply by psychic force. Ruth would agree with him at least in this case, for she didn't seem to like Harvey, try as she might. It had already got to the point that everything Harvey did and said, if it was only good night, to her mind made him worse and worse. It was true there are ways and ways of saying good night. Yet Edward wondered if there wasn't something of demonology in those confidences he shared with Ruth about Harvey; Ruth didn't know him as well as Edward did. They had certainly built up a case against Harvey between themselves which they wouldn't have aired openly. It was for this reason that Edward had thought it fair that he should come alone, although at first he expected Ruth to come with him. She had said she couldn't face it. Perhaps, Edward had thought, I might be more fair to Harvey.

And yet, here he was, sitting in the car before his

house, noting how the grass everywhere else was greener than that immediately surrounding the cottage. Edward got out and slammed the door with a bang, hoping to provoke the dark front door of the house or at least one of the windows into action. He went to the gate. It was closed with a rusty wire loop which he loosened. He creaked open the gate and walked up the path to the door and knocked. It was ten past three, and Harvey was expecting him; it had all been arranged. But he knocked and there was silence. This, too, was typical. He walked round the back of the house, looking for a car or a motor-cycle, which he supposed Harvey had. He found there a wide path, a sort of drive which led away from the back door, through the woods; this path had been hidden from the main road. There was no motor-cycle, but a newish small Renault, light brown, under a rush-covered shelter. Harvey, then, was probably at home. The back door was his front door, so Edward banged on that. Harvey opened it immediately and stood with that look of his, to the effect that he had done his utmost.

"You haven't cut your hair," he said.

Edward had the answer ready, heated up from the pre-cooking, so many times had he told Harvey much the same thing. "It's my hair, not your hair. It's my beard, not your beard." Edward stepped into the house as he said this, so that Harvey had to make way for him.

Harvey was predictable only up to a point. "What are you trying to prove, Edward," he said, "wearing that poncho at your age?" In the living room he pushed some chairs out of the way. "And your hair hanging down your back," he said.

Edward's hair was in fact shoulder-length. "I'm growing it for a part in a film," he said, then wished he hadn't given any excuse at all since anyway it was his hair, not Harvey's hair. Red hair.

"You've got a part?"

"Yes."

"What are you doing here, then? Why aren't you rehearsing?"

"Rehearsals start on Monday."

"Where?"

"Elstree."

"Elstree." Harvey said it as if there was a third party listening—as if to draw the attention of this third party to that definite word, Elstree, and whatever connotations it might breed.

Edward wished himself back in time by twenty minutes, driving along the country road from St. Dié to Nancy, feeling the spring weather. The spring weather, the cherry trees in flower, and all the budding green on the road from St. Dié had supported him, while here inside Harvey's room there was no outward support. He almost said, "What am I doing here?" but refrained because that would be mere rhetoric. He had come about his sister-in-law Effie, Harvey's wife.

"Your wire was too long," said Harvey. "You could have saved five words."

"I can see you're busy," said Edward.

Effie was very far from Edward's heart of hearts, but Ruth worried about her. Long ago he'd had an affair with beautiful Effie, but that was a thing of the past. He had come here for Ruth's sake. He reminded himself carefully that he would do almost anything for Ruth.

"What's the act?" said Harvey. "You are somehow not yourself, Edward."

It seemed to Edward that Harvey always suspected him of putting on an act.

"Maybe I can speak for actors in general; that, I don't know," Edward said. "But I suppose that the nature of my profession is mirrored in my own experience; at least, for certain, I can speak for myself. That, I can most certainly do. In fact I know when I'm playing a part and when I'm not. It isn't every actor who knows the difference. The majority act better off stage than on."

Edward went into the little sitting room that Harvey had put together, the minimum of stuff to keep him going while he did the job he had set himself. Indeed, the shabby, green plush chairs with the stuffing coming out of them and the quite small work-table with the papers and writing materials piled on it (he wrote by hand) seemed out of all proportion to the project. Harvey was only studying a subject, preparing an essay, a thesis. Why all this spectacular neglect of material things? God knows, thought Edward, from where he has collected his furniture. There was a kitchen visible beyond the room, with a loaf of bread and a coffee mug on the table. It looked like a nineteenth-century narrative painting. Edward supposed there were habitable rooms upstairs. He sat down when Harvey told him to. From where he sat he could see through a window a washing-line with baby clothes on it. There was no sign of a baby in the house, so Edward presumed this washing had nothing to do with Harvey; maybe it belonged to a daily help who brought along her child's clothes to wash.

Harvey said, "I'm awfully busy."

"I've come about Effie," Edward said.

Harvey took a long time to respond. This, thought Edward, is a habit of his when he wants an effect of weightiness.

Then, "Oh, Effie," said Harvey, looking suddenly relieved; he actually began to smile as if to say he had feared to be confronted with some problem that really counted.

Harvey had written Effie off that time on the Italian *autostrada* about a year ago, when they were driving from Bologna to Florence—Ruth, Edward, Effie, Harvey and Nathan, a young student-friend of Ruth's. They had stopped for a refill of petrol; Effie and Ruth went off to the Ladies', then they came back to the car where it was still waiting in line. It was a cool, late afternoon in April, rather cloudy, not one of those hot Italian days where you feel you must have a cold drink or an ice every time you stop. It was sheer consumerism that made Harvey—or maybe it was Nathan—suggest that they should go and get something from the snack-bar; this was a big catering monopoly with huge windows in which were arranged straw baskets and pottery from Hong Kong and fantastically shaped bottles of Italian liqueurs. It was, "What shall we have from the bar?"—"A sandwich, a coffee?"—"No, I don't want any more of those lousy sandwiches." Effie went off to see what there was to buy, and came back with some chocolate.—"Yes, that's what I'd like."—She had two large bars. The tank was now full. Edward paid the man at the pump. Effie got in the front with him. They were all in the car and Edward drove off. Effie started dividing the chocolate and handing it round. Nathan, Ruth and Harvey at the back, all took a piece. Edward took a piece and Effie started eating her piece.

With her mouth full of chocolate she turned and said to Harvey at the back, "It's good, isn't it? I stole it. Have another piece."

"You what?" said Harvey. Ruth said something, too, to the same effect. Edward said he didn't believe it.

Effie said, "Why shouldn't we help ourselves? These multinationals and monopolies are capitalizing on us, and two-thirds of the world is suffering." She tore open the second slab, crammed more chocolate angrily into her mouth, and, with her mouth gluttonously full of stolen chocolate, went on raving about how two-thirds of the world was starving.

"You make it worse for them and worse for all of us if you steal," Edward said.

"That's right," said Ruth, "it really does make it worse for everyone. Besides, it's dishonest."

"Well, I don't know," Nathan said.

But Harvey didn't wait to hear more. "Pull in at the side," he said. They were going at a hundred kilometres an hour, but he had his hand on the back door on the dangerous side of the road. Edward pulled in. He forgot, now, how it was that they reasoned Harvey out of leaving the car there on the *autostrada;* however, he sat in silence while Effie ate her chocolate, inveighing, meanwhile, against the capitalist system. None of the others would accept any more of the chocolate. Just before the next exit Harvey said, "Pull in here, I want to pee." They waited for him while he went to the men's lavatory. Edward was suspicious all along that he wouldn't come back and when the minutes went by he got out of the car to have a look, and was just in time to see Harvey get up into a truck beside the driver; away he went.

They lost the truck at some point along the road, after they reached Florence. Harvey's disappearance ruined Effie's holiday. She was furious, and went on against him so much that Ruth made that always infuriating point: "If he's so bad, why are you angry with him for leaving you?" The rest of them were upset and uneasy for a day or two but after that they let it go. After all, they were on holiday. Edward refused to discuss the subject for the next two weeks; they were travelling along the Tuscan coast stopping here and there. It would have been a glorious trip but for Effie's fury and unhappiness.

Up to the time Edward went to see Harvey in France on her behalf, she still hadn't seen any more of him. They had no children and he had simply left her life, with all his possessions and the electricity bills and other clutter of married living on her hands. All over a bit of chocolate. And yet, no.

Ruth thought, and Edward agreed with her, that a lot must have led up to that final parting of Harvey from Effie.

Edward deeply envied Harvey, he didn't know exactly what for. Or rather, perhaps he had better not probe deeply enough into the possibility that if Ruth wasn't Ruth and, if they weren't always so much in agreement, he would have liked to walk off, just like that. When Harvey talked of his marriage it was always as if he were thinking of something else, and he never talked about it unless someone else did first. And then, it was as if the other person had mentioned something quite irrelevant to his life, provoking from him a puzzled look, then a frown, an effort of concentration, it seemed, then an impatient dismissal of the apparently alien subject. It seemed, it seemed, Edward thought; because one can only judge by appearances. How could Edward know Harvey wasn't putting on an act, as he so often implied that Edward did? To some extent we all put on acts.

Harvey began to be more sociable, for he had somehow dismissed the subject of Effie. He must have known Edward would bring up Effie later, that in fact all he had come for was to talk about her. Well, perhaps not all. Edward was an old friend. Harvey poured him a drink, and, for the moment, Edward gave up trying to get on to the subject of Effie.

"Tell me," said Harvey, "about the new film. What's it called? What sort of part are you playing?"

"It's called *The Love-Hate Relationship*. That's only provisional as a title. I don't think it'll sell as a film on that title. But it's based on a novel called *The Love-Hate Relationship*. And that's what the film is about. There's a married couple and another man, a brother, in the middle. I'm playing the other man, the brother." (Was Harvey listening? He was looking round into the other room.)

"If there's anything I can't stand it's a love-hate relationship," Harvey said turning back to Edward at last. "The element of love in such a relation simply isn't worthy of the name. It boils down to hatred pure and simple in the end. Love comprises among other things a desire for the well-being and spiritual freedom of the one who is loved. There's an objective quality about love. Love-hate is obsessive, it is possessive. It can be evil in effect."

"Oh well," Edward said, "love-hate is a frequent human problem. It's a very important problem, you can't deny it."

"It's part of the greater problem," said Harvey after a while. Edward knew what Harvey was coming round to and was pleased, now that he was sitting here with his drink and his old friend. It was the problem of suffering as it is dealt with in the biblical *Book of Job.* It was, for this, in the first place, that Harvey had come to study here in the French countryside away from the environment of his family business and his friends.

Harvey was a rich man; he was in his mid-thirties. He had started writing a monograph about the *Book of Job* and the problem it deals with. For he could not face that a benevolent Creator, one whose charming and delicious light descended and spread over the world, and being powerful everywhere, could condone the unspeakable sufferings of the world; that God did permit all suffering and was therefore, by logic of his omnipotence, the actual author of it, he was at a loss how to square with the existence of God, given the premise that God is good.

"It is the only problem," Harvey had always said. Now, Harvey believed in God, and this was what tormented him. "It's the only problem, in fact, worth discussing."

It was just under a year after Harvey had disappeared that Effie traced him to St. Dié. She hadn't been to see him herself, but she had written several times through

his lawyer asking him what was the matter. She described to him the process by which she had tracked him
down; when she read Edward the letter before she posted
it he felt she could have left that part out, for she had
traced him quite simply, but by trickery, of which
Harvey would not see the charm; furthermore, her reve-
lation of the trick compromised an innocent, if foolish,
person, and this fact would not be lost on Harvey. His
moral sense was always intensified where Effie was concerned.

"Don't tell him, Effie," Edward said, "how you got his
address. He'll think you unprincipled."

"He thinks that already," she said.

"Well, this might be the finishing touch. There's no
need to tell."

"I don't want him back."

"You only want his money," Edward said.

"Oh, God, Edward, if you only knew what he was like
to live with."

Edward could guess. But he said, "What people are
like to live with . . . It isn't a good test to generalize
on."

"He's rich," said Effie. "He's spoilt." Effie had a lover,
Ernie Howe, an electronics expert. Effie was very good-
looking and it was hardly to be expected that she would
resist, year after year, the opportunities for love affairs
that came her way all the time; she was really beautiful.
Ernie Howe was a nice-looking man, too, but he lacked
the sort of money Harvey had and Effie was used to.
Ernie had his job, and quite a good one; Edward supposed
that Effie, who herself had a job with an advertising firm,
might have been content with the simpler life with him,
if she was in love with Ernie. It was only that now she

23

was expecting a baby she felt she might persuade Harvey to divorce her with a large settlement. Edward didn't see why this should not be.

Harvey had never replied to any of Effie's letters. She continued to write, care of his lawyer. She told him of her love affair and mentioned a divorce.

Finally she managed to find his actual whereabouts in St. Dié, in a quite unpremeditated way. She had in fact visited the lawyer to try to persuade him to reveal the address. He answered that he could only forward a letter. Effie went home and wrote a letter, calling with it at the lawyer's office the next day to save the extra time it would have taken in the post. She gave it to the receptionist and asked that it be forwarded. There were two or three letters on the girl's desk, in a neat pile, already stamped. Acting on a brainwave Effie said, casually, "If you like, as I'm passing the post box, I'll pop them all in."

"Oh, thanks," said the foolish girl, "I have to go beyond the bus stop to post letters." So she hastily filled in Harvey's address and handed the letters to Effie with a smile. And although Edward said to Effie, "You shouldn't tell Harvey how you got his address. It'll put him right off. Counterproductive. And rather unfair on the poor girl at the lawyer's office," she went ahead and wrote to Harvey direct, telling him of her little trick. "He'll realize all the more how urgent it is," she said.

But still Harvey didn't reply.

That was how Edward came to be on this errand to Harvey on her behalf. Incidentally, Edward also hoped for a loan. He was short of money till he got paid under his contract with the film people.

Edward used to confide in Harvey, and he in Edward, during their student life together. Harvey had never, to Edward's knowledge, broken any of these confidences in the sense of revealing them to other people; but he had a way of playing them back to Edward at inopportune moments; it was disconcerting, it made Edward uncomfortable, especially as Harvey chose to remind him of things he had said which he would rather have forgotten. Harvey seemed especially to choose the negative remarks he made all those years ago, ten, twelve, years ago, such as when he had said something unfavourable about Ruth, something that sounded witty, perhaps, at the time, but which he probably didn't mean. Scarcely ever did Harvey remind him of the praise he devoted in sincere abundance to others, Ruth included. So many sweet things seemed to have spilled out of his ears as soon as they entered them; so many of the sour and the sharp, the unripe and frivolously carping observations he made, Harvey had saved up in his memory-bank at compound interest; it seemed to Edward that he capitalized on these past confidences at a time when they were likely to have the most deflating effect on him; he called this a breach of confidence in a very special sense. Harvey would deny this, of course; he would claim that he had a clear memory, that his reminders were salutary, that Edward was inclined to fool himself, and that the uncomfortable truths of the past were always happier in their outcome than convenient illusions.

And undoubtedly Harvey was often right. That he had a cold side was no doubt a personal matter. In Edward's view it wasn't incompatible with Harvey's extremely good mind and his occasional flashes of generosity. And indeed his moral judgment. Perhaps a bit too much moral judgment.

Edward always spoke a lot about himself and Harvey as they were in their young days, even to people who didn't know them. But few people listen carefully to the reminiscences of someone who has achieved nothing much in life; the end-product of a personal record has somehow to justify the telling. What did come across to Edward's friends was that he had Harvey more or less on his mind. Edward wished something to happen in his own life to make him forget Harvey, get his influence out of his system. Only some big change in my life could do that, Edward thought. Divorce from Ruth, which was unthinkable (then how did I come to think it?). Or great success as an actor; something I haven't got.

Eventually Edward said, as he sat in Harvey's cottage in France, "I've come about Effie, mainly. Ruth's anxious about her, very anxious. I've come here for Ruth's sake."

"I recall," Harvey said, "how you told me once, when you first married Ruth, 'Ruth is a curate's wife and always will be.' "

Edward was disconcerted. "Oh, I was only putting on an act. You know how it was in those days."

In those days Edward had been a curate, doing so well with church theatricals that he was in demand from other parishes up and down the country. It wasn't so very long before he realized he was an actor, not a curate, not a vicar in bud. Only his sermons interested him and that was because he had his own little stage up there in the pulpit, and an audience. The congregation loved his voice and his delivery. When he resigned, what they said mostly in their letters was, "You were always so genuine in your sermons," and "One knew you felt every word." Well, in fact Edward was and did. But in fact he was more involved in the delivery of his sermons than in the substance. He said good-bye to the fund-raising performances of *The Admirable Crichton* and *The Silver Box*, not to mention *A Midsummer Night's Dream* on the one chilly midsummer night when he was a curate.

He had played parts in repertory theatre, then that principal part (in *The Curate's Egg*) in the West End, and was well launched in his film career, spasmodic and limited though it was, by the time he sat talking to Harvey on Effie's behalf, largely for Ruth's sake. To himself, Edward now described his acting career as "limited" in the sense that too often he had been cast as a clergyman, an unfrocked priest or a welfare worker. But, at present, in the film provisionally entitled *The Love-Hate Relationship*, he had been cast in a different role, to his great pleasure; he was playing a sardonic scholar, a philosopher. Thinking himself into the part had made him feel extraordinarily equal to his discussion with Harvey; and he returned, with the confidence of the part, to the subject of Effie.

"She wants a divorce," he said, and waited the inevitable few seconds for Harvey's reply.

"Nothing to stop her."

"She wants to get married, she's expecting a baby by Ernie Howe. And you know very well she's written to you about it."

"What she wrote to me about was money. She wants money to get married with. I'm a busy man with things to do. Money; not enough money but a lot. That's what Effie boils down to."

"Oh, not entirely. I should have thought you wanted her to be happy. After all, you left her. You left Effie abruptly."

Harvey waited a while. Time was not of an essence, here. "Well, she soon found consolation. But she can get a divorce quite easily. Ernie Howe has a job."

Edward said, "I don't know if you realize how hateful you can be, Harvey. If it wasn't for your money you wouldn't speak like that." For it struck him that, since Harvey had recently come into a vast share of a Canadian uncle's fortune, he ought not to carry on as if he were the moderately well-off Harvey of old. This treatment of Effie was brutal.

"I don't know what you mean," said Harvey, in his time. "I really don't care what you mean, what you say. I'll give you a letter to Stewart Cowper, my lawyer in London, with suitable instructions." Harvey got up and reached on a bookshelf for a block of writing paper and one envelope. He said, "I'll write it now. Then you can go away."

He wrote without much reflection, almost as if he had come to an earlier decision about the paying off of Effie, and by how much, and had just been waiting for the moment Edward arrived to make a settlement. He addressed the envelope, put in the folded letter, then sealed it down. He handed it to Edward. "You can take it straight to him yourself. Quicker than posting it."

Edward was astonished that Harvey had sealed the letter since he was to be the bearer. Bloody indelicate. He wondered why Harvey was trying to diminish him.

"Harvey," he said, "are you putting on an act? Are

you playing the part of a man who's a swine merely because he can afford to be?"

Harvey took a lot of thought. Then, "Yes," he said.

"Well, it doesn't suit you. One meets that sort of character amongst the older generation of the motion picture and theatre world. I remember hearing a producer say to a script writer, 'It's the man who writes the cheque who has the final say in the script. And I'm the man who writes the cheque.' One still hears that sort of thing. He had yellow eye-balls."

Harvey sat with folded arms staring at his loaded work-table.

"I suppose you're playing this part to relieve your feelings?" Edward said.

"I imagine you are relieving yours, Edward."

"I suppose you're fairly disgusted with things," Edward said. "With Effie and so on. I know you left her that day in disgust when she was eating her stolen chocolate and talking about the sufferings of the hungry. All that. But Effie has some good points, you know. Some very good points."

"If you want a loan why don't you ask for it?" Harvey said, staring at his papers as if nostalgic for their lonely company.

Anxiety, suffering, were recorded in his face; that was certain. Edward wasn't sure that this was not self-induced. Harvey had once said, "There can be only one answer to the question of why people suffer, irrespective of whether they are innocent or guilty; to the question of why suffering has no relation to the moral quality of the individual, of the tribe or of the nation, one way or another. If you believe that there is a Creator, a God, and that he is good, the only logical answer to the problem of suffering is that the individual soul has made a pact with God before he is born, that he will suffer during his lifetime. We are born forgetful of this pact, of course; but we have made it. Sufferers would, in this hypothesis, be pre-conscious volunteers. The same might apply to tribes or nations, especially in the past."

Edward had been very impressed by this, by then the latest, idea of Harvey's. (How many ideas about *Job* they had formulated in the past!) But he had said he still couldn't see the need for suffering.

"Oh, development involves suffering," Harvey had said.

"I wonder if I made that agreement with God before I was born," said Edward at that time, "for I've suffered."

"We have all suffered," said Harvey, "but I'm talking about the great multitudes who are starving to death every year, for instance. The glaze-eyed infants."

"Could your theory be borne out by science?"

"I think possibly there might be a genetic interpretation of it. But I'm talking theologically."

When, now, Edward looked at his friend's face and saw stress on it, rich and authoritative as Harvey was, swine as he could be, he envied him for the detachment with which he was able to set himself to working on the problem through the *Book of Job*. It was possible for a man like Harvey to be detached and involved at the same time. As an actor, Edward envied him. He also envied the ease with which he could write to his lawyer about his divorce from Effie without a thought for the money involved. As for Edward's loan, Harvey had already written a cheque without a word, knowing, of course, that Edward would pay it back in time. And then, although Harvey wasn't consistently generous, and had ignored Effie's letters, Edward remembered how only a few months ago he had arranged bail through his ever-ready lawyer for Effie and Ruth's student, Nathan, when they were arrested during a demonstration and been had up for riot and affray. Effie didn't need the bail money, for her lover came to the rescue first, but Nathan did. They were both bound over to keep the peace. Harvey's money was so casual. Edward envied him that, and felt guilty, glimpsing again, for that sharp unthinkable instant, the possibility that he might like to part from Ruth as abruptly and as easily. Edward closed the subject in his mind quickly, very quickly. It had been established that Ruth and Edward always thought alike. Edward didn't want to dwell on that thought, either.

As a theological student Edward had spent many an hour lying with Harvey Gotham on the grass in the great green university square if the weather was fine in the early summer, while the croquet mallets clicked on another part of the green, and the croquet players' voices made slight exclamations, and together he and Harvey discussed the *Book of Job*, which they believed was not only as important, as amazing, a poem as it was generally considered to be, but also the pivotal book of the Bible.

Edward had always maintained that the link—or should he say fetter?—that first bound him to Harvey was their deep old love of marvellous Job, their studies, their analyses, their theories. Harvey used to lie on his back on the grass, one leg stretched out, the other bent at the knee, while Edward sat by his side sunning his face and contemplating the old castle, while he listened with another part of his mind to Harvey's talk. "It is the only problem. The problem of suffering is the only problem. It all boils down to that."

"Did you know," Edward remembered saying, "that when Job was finally restored to prosperity and family abundance, one of his daughters was called Box of Eye-Paint? Can we really imagine our tormented hero enjoying his actual reward?"

"No," said Harvey. "He continued to suffer."

"Not according to the Bible."

"Still, I'm convinced he suffered on. Perhaps more."

"It seems odd, doesn't it," Edward had said, "after he sat on a dung-heap and suffered from skin sores and put up with his friends' gloating, and lost his family and his cattle, that he should have to go on suffering."

"It became a habit," Harvey said, "for he not only argued the problem of suffering, he suffered the problem of argument. And that is incurable."

"But he wanted to argue with God."

"Yes, but God as a character comes out badly, very badly. Thunder and bluster and I'm Me, who are you? Putting on an act. Behold now Leviathan. Behold now Behemoth. Ha, ha among the trumpets. Where wast thou when I laid the foundations of the earth? And Job, insincerely and wrongly, says, 'I am vile.' And God says, all right, that being understood, I give you back double your goods, you can have fourteen thousand sheep and six thousand camels and a thousand yoke of oxen, and a thousand she-asses. And seven sons and three daughters. The third daughter was Keren-happuch—that was Eye-Paint."

Towards evening, on the day when Edward visited Harvey at his place near St. Dié, Harvey went out and brought in the baby clothes. He didn't fold them; he just dumped them on a chair in the little scullery at the back of the kitchen. He seemed to forget that he was impatient for Edward to leave. He brought out some wine, some glasses, cheese and bread. In fact, Edward could see that Harvey didn't want him to leave, lest he should feel lonely afterwards. Edward had been feeling rather guilty at interrupting what was probably a fairly contented solitude. Now, it was not that he regretted imposing his presence, but that by doing so he must impose the absence to follow. For Harvey more and more seemed to want him to remain. Edward said something about catching a night ferry. He thought, Surely Harvey's involved with the mother of the baby whose clothes he's just brought in off the line. They must be the clothes of an infant not more than a year old. Where are the mother and child?

There was no sign of any mother or child apart from the clothes Harvey had dumped on a chair. Edward was envious, too. He was envious of Harvey's woman and his child. He wanted, at that moment, to be free like Harvey and to have a girl somewhere, but not visible, with a baby.

Harvey said, "It's fairly lonely here." By which Edward knew for certain that Harvey was suddenly very lonely indeed at the thought of his leaving. The mother and child were probably away for the night.

"Stay the night," said Harvey. "There's plenty of room."

Edward wanted to know where Harvey had been and what he'd been doing since he disappeared on the *autostrada*. But they did not talk of that. Harvey told him that Effie was writing a thesis on child-labourers in the Western democracies, basing much of it on Kingsley's *The Water Babies*. She hadn't told Edward this. Harvey seemed pleased that he had a bit more news of her than Edward had. But then they had a laugh over Effie and her zeal in the sociological industry.

Harvey made up a bed for him in a sort of cupboard-room upstairs. It was nearly four in the morning when he pulled the extra rough covers over a mattress and piled two cushions for a pillow. From the doorway into Harvey's bedroom Edward could see that the bed was narrow, the furniture quite spare in a cheap new way. He said, "Where's the baby?"

"What baby?" Harvey said.

"The baby whose washing was out on the line."

"Oh that," said Harvey; "that's only my safeguard. I put baby clothes out on the line every day and bring them in at night. I change the clothes every other day, naturally."

Edward wondered if Harvey had really gone mad.

"Well, I don't understand," Edward said, turning away as if it didn't matter.

"You see," said Harvey, "the police don't break in and shoot if there's likely to be a baby inside. Otherwise they might just break in and shoot."

"Go to hell," Edward said.

"Well if I told you the truth you wouldn't understand."

"Thanks," he said.

"You wouldn't believe," said Harvey.

"All right, I don't want to know."

"When I settled here I strung up the clothes-line. I have a sure system of keeping away the well-meaning women who always come round a lone man, wanting to cook and launder and mend socks and do the shopping; they love a bachelor; even in cities—no trouble at all getting domestic help for a single man. In my wanderings since I left Effie I've always found that a line of baby clothes, varying from day to day, keeps these solicitous women away; they imagine, without thinking more of it, that there's already a woman around."

But Edward knew him too well; it was surely one of those demonstrative acts by which Harvey attempted to communicate with a world whose intelligence he felt was away behind his own. Harvey was always in a state of exasperation, and, it was true, always ten thoughts ahead of everybody around him. Always likely to be outrageous. The baby clothes probably belonged to his girl.

Edward left three hours later before Harvey was up. He still felt envious of Harvey for his invisible and probably non-existent girl and her baby.

II

Nathan fox was sitting up with Ruth when Edward got back to London. It was a Sunday, a Pimlico Sunday with vacant parking spaces and lights in some of the windows.

Nathan had graduated in English literature, at the university where Ruth was now teaching, over a year before. He couldn't get a job. Ruth looked after him most of the time. Edward always said he himself would do almost anything for Ruth; they saw eye to eye. So Nathan was quite welcome. But just that night on his return from France, very tired, and needing to get to bed for an early rise the next morning—he was due at the studio at seven—just that night Edward wished Nathan Fox wasn't there. Edward was not at all sure how they would manage without Nathan. Nathan wasn't ashamed of calling himself an intellectual, which, for people like themselves, made life so much easier; not that he was, in fact, an intellectual, really; he was only educated. But they could talk to Nathan about anything; and at the same time he made himself useful in the house. Indeed, he was a very fair cook. To a working couple like Ruth and Edward he was an invaluable friend.

It was just that night, and on a few previous occasions, Edward wished he wasn't there. Edward wanted to talk to Ruth, to get to bed early. Nathan sat there in his tight jeans and his T-shirt with "Poetry Is Emotion Recollected In Tranquillity" printed on it. He was a good-looking boy, tall, with an oval face, very smooth and rather silvery-green in colour—really olive. His eyebrows were smooth, black and arched, his hair heavy and sleek, quite black. But he wasn't vain at all. He got up in the morning, took a shower, shaved and dressed, all in less than seven minutes. It seemed to Edward that the alarm in their room had only just gone off when he could smell the coffee brewing in the kitchen, and hear Nathan already setting the places for breakfast. Ruth, too, wondered how he managed it. His morning smile was delightful; he had a mouth like a Michelangelo angel and teeth so good, clear, strong and shapely it seemed to Edward, secretly, that they were the sexiest thing about him.

The only problem with Nathan was how to explain what he saw in them. They paid him and fed him as well as they could, but it was supposed to be only a fill-in job. They were together as on a North Sea oil platform. It wasn't that Nathan wouldn't leave them, it now seemed he couldn't. Edward thought, He is hankering after Effie, and we are the nearest he can get to her. Edward often wondered whether Effie would really marry Ernie Howe when she got her divorce from Harvey.

When Edward got back from France they had supper; he told Nathan and Ruth what had happened at Harvey's cottage, almost from start to finish. Ruth wanted actually to see with her eyes the sealed letter to the lawyer; so Edward got up from the table and fished it out of his duffel bag.

She turned it over and over in her hand; she examined it closely; she almost smelt it. She said, "How rude to seal down a letter you were to carry by hand."

"Why?" said Nathan.

"Because one doesn't," Ruth piped primly, "seal letters that other people are to carry."

"What about the postman?"

"Oh, I mean one's friends."

"Well, open it," said Nathan.

Edward had been rather hoping he would suggest this, and he knew Ruth had the same idea in mind. If they'd been alone, neither of them would have suggested it out loud, although it would certainly have occurred to them, so eager were they to know what Harvey had settled on Effie in this letter to his solicitors. They would have left the letter and their secret desires unopened. They were still somewhat of the curate and his wife, Ruth and himself.

But Nathan seemed to serve them like a gentleman who takes a high hand in matters of form, or an unselfconscious angel. In a way, that is what he was there for, if he had to be there. He often said things out of his inexperience and cheerful ignorance that they themselves wanted to say but did not dare.

"Open it?" said Ruth.

"Oh, we can't do that," said Edward.

"You can steam it open," suggested Nathan, as if they didn't know. "You only need a kettle."

"Really?" said Ruth.

Nathan proceeded, very know-all: "It won't be noticed. You can seal it up again. My mother steamed open my aunt's letters. Only wanted to know what was in them, that's all. Then later my aunt would tell a lot of lies about what was in the letters, but my mother knew the truth, of course. That was after my father died, and my mother and my auntie were living together."

"I don't know that we have the right," said Ruth.

"It's your duty," Nathan pronounced. He turned to Edward, appealing: "In my mother's case it wasn't a duty, although she said it was. But in your case it's definitely a duty to steam open that letter. It might be dynamite you've been carrying."

Edward said, "He should have left it open. It might be really offensive or something. It was ill-mannered of Harvey. I noticed it at the time, in fact."

"You should have objected," Nathan said. Edward was now delighted that Nathan was there with them that evening.

"It's difficult to object," Ruth said. "But I think we have a right to know what's in it. At least you do, Edward, since you're the bearer."

They steamed open the letter in the kitchen and stood reading it together.

Dear Stewart,

This letter is being brought to you by Edward Jansen, an old friend of mine from university days.

I don't know if you've met him. He's a sort of actor but that is by the way. My wife Effie is his sister-in-law. He came to see me about Effie's divorce. As you know I'm not contesting it. She wants a settlement. Let her go on wanting, let her sue.

The object of this letter is to tell you that I agree the date of *Job* is post-exile, that is, about 500 B.C. but it could be the middle of the 5th century. It could easily be contemporaneous with the *Prometheus Bound* of Aeschylus. (The *Philoctetes* of Sophocles, another *Job*-style work, is dated I think about 409.)

Yours,
Harvey

"I won't deliver it," Edward said.

"Oh, you must," said Nathan. "You mustn't let him think you've opened it."

"There's something fishy about it," Edward said. He was greatly annoyed.

"Calling you a sort of actor," Ruth said, in a soothing voice that made him nearly choleric.

"It's Effie's fault," said Ruth. "She's brought out this quality in Harvey."

"Well, I'm too busy tomorrow to go in person to Gray's Inn," Edward said.

"I'll deliver it," said Nathan.

III

It was october. Harvey sat at his writing-table, set against the wall of the main room in his little house.

"*Job* 37:5," he wrote, "God thundereth marvellously with his voice . . ."

"I think we'll have to send to England for some more cretonne fabric," said Ruth, looking over his shoulder.

It was at the end of August that Ruth had moved in, bringing with her Effie's baby, a girl. The baby was now asleep for a merciful moment, upstairs.

Harvey looked up from his work. "I try to exude good-will," he said.

"You positively try to sweat it," Ruth said, kindly. And she wondered how it was that she had disliked and resented Harvey for so many years. It still amazed her to find herself here with him. That he was perfectly complacent about the arrangement, even cheerful and happy, did not surprise her so much; everything around him, she knew—all the comings and goings—were really peripheral to his preoccupation with the *Book of Job*. But her being there, with Effie's baby, astonished her sometimes to the point of vertigo. This was not at all what she had planned when she decided to turn up at the cottage with Effie's baby daughter.

Once, after she had settled in, she said to Harvey, "I didn't plan this."

"It wasn't a plan," said Harvey, "it was a plot."

"I suppose it looks like that from the outside," Ruth said. To her, what she had wanted was justice. Given Effie's character, it was not to be expected that she would continue to live with Ernie Howe on his pay in a small house. Ruth had offered to take the baby when Effie decided she wasn't in love with Ernie any more. Harvey's money would perhaps not have made much difference to Effie's decision. At any rate, Ruth had known that, somehow, in the end, she would have to take on Effie's baby. It rather pleased her.

Effie was trying to sue Harvey for alimony, so far, without success. "The lawyers are always on the side of the money," she said. Harvey continued to ignore her letters.

The baby, named Clara, was born toward the end of June. Effie went back to her job in advertising for a short while after she had left Ernie Howe. Then she took a job with an international welfare organization in Rome. Ernie wasn't at all happy, at first, with Ruth's plan to take the baby Clara to visit Harvey. They sat in the flat in Pimlico where Ernie often came, now, for consolation, as much as to see his daughter.

"He doesn't sound the sort of man to have any *sent-y-ments,*" Ernie said.

Edward wanted very much to give Ernie some elocution lessons to restore his voice to the plain tones of his origins. "He hasn't any sentimentality, but of course he has sentiments," said Edward.

"Especially about his wife's baby by a, well, a lover."

"As to that," said Edward, "he won't care who the father is. He just won't have any sentimental feelings, full stop."

"It's a matter of justice," Ruth said.

"How do you work that out?" said Nathan.

"Well, if it hadn't been for Harvey leaving Effie she would never have had a baby by Ernie," Ruth said. "Harvey should have given her a child. So Harvey's responsible for Clara; it's a question of justice, and with all his riches it would be the best thing if he could take responsibility, pay Effie her alimony. He might even take Effie back."

"Effie doesn't want to go back to Harvey Gotham," said Ernie.

"Harvey won't take her back," Edward said. "He believes that Effie boils down to money."

"Alas, he's right," said Ernie.

"Why can't Clara go on living with us?" said Nathan, who already knew how to prepare the feeds and bath the baby.

"I'm only taking her for a visit," Ruth said. "What's wrong with that? You went to see Harvey, Edward. Now I'll have a try."

"Be sure to bring her back, Ree-uth," said Ernie. "The legal position—"

"Do you still want to marry Effie?" Edward asked him.

"No, quite frankly, I don't."

"Effie's so beautiful," Nathan said. He got up to replenish the drinks. "What a beautiful girl she is!"

"A matter of justice. A balancing of accounts." This was how Ruth put it to Harvey. "I'm passionate about justice," she said.

"People who want justice," Harvey said, "generally want so little when it comes to the actuality. There is more to be had from the world than a balancing of accounts."

She supposed he was thinking of his character Job, as in fact he was. She was used to men answering her with one part of their mind on religion. That was one of the reasons why Edward had become so unsatisfactory after he had ceased to be a curate and become an actor.

Ruth and Effie grew up in a country rectory that today is converted into four commodious flats. The shabbiness of the war still hung over it in the late fifties, but they were only aware of the general decay by the testimony of their elders as to how things were "in the old days," and the evidence of pre-war photographs of garden parties where servants and trees stood about, welltended, and the drawing room chintzes were well-fitted and new. Otherwise, they simply accepted that life was a muddle of broken barrows, tin buckets in the garden sheds, overgrown gardens, neglected trees. They had an oak of immense girth; a mulberry tree older than the house, to judge from early sketches of the place. The graveyard had a yew the circumference and shape of their oval dining-table; the tree was hollow inside and the bark had formed itself into the shape of organ pipes. Yews were planted in graveyards, originally, because they poisoned cattle, and as they were needed for long-bows they were planted in a place where cattle didn't go. All this Ruth picked up from God knows where; the air she breathed informed her. House-martens nested under the eaves outside Ruth's room and used to make a dark-and-white flash almost up to the open window as they came and fled in the morning.

There was a worn carpet on the staircase up to the first landing. After that, bare wood. Most of the rooms were simply shut for ever. They had been civil servants' bedrooms in war-time before Ruth was born, and she never knew what it was like to see the houseful of people that the rectory was made for.

For most of Ruth's life, up to the time Edward became an actor, religion was her bread and butter. Her father was what Edward at one time called a career-Christian; she assumed he was a believer too, as was her mother; but she never got the impression that either had time to think about it.

Effie was three years younger than Ruth. The sisters were very close to each other all their schooldays and in their early twenties. Ruth often wondered when exactly they had separated in their attitude to life. It was probably after Ruth's return from Paris where she had spent a year with a family. Shortly afterwards Effie, too, went off to be an *au pair* in France.

If you are the child of a doctor or a butcher you don't

have to believe in your father's occupation. But, in their childhood, they had to believe in their father's job as a clergyman in a special way. Matins and Sunday services and Evensong were part of the job; the family was officially poor, which was to say they were not the poor in the streets and cottages, but poor by the standards of a country rector. Ruth's mother was a free-lance typist and always had some work in hand. She could do seventy words a minute on her old pre-war typewriter. Before her marriage she had done a hundred and thirty words a minute at Pitman's shorthand. Ruth used to go to sleep on a summer night hearing the tap-tapping of the typewriter below, and wake to the almost identical sound of the woodpecker in the tree outside her window. Ruth supposed this was Effie's experience too, but when she reminded her sister of it many years later Effie couldn't recall any sound effects.

Effie went to a university on her return from France and left after her first year about the time that Ruth graduated and married Edward. Ruth worked with and for Edward and the parish, organizing a live crib at Christmas with a real baby, a real cow and a real virgin; she wrote special prayers to the Holy Spirit and the Trinity for the parish magazine (which she described as Prayers to the H.S. etc.) and she arranged bring-and-pay garden lunches. She lectured and made bedspreads, and she taught child-welfare and jam preserving. Ruth was very much in the business. Effie, meanwhile, went off the rails, and when this was pointed out to her in so many words, she said, "What rails? Whose rails?" It was Effie who first called Edward an actor more than a man of God, and she probably put the idea in his mind.

Effie was doing social work when Ruth got married.

The sisters looked very much alike in their separate features; it was one of those cases where the sum total of each came out with a difference, to the effect that Effie was extremely beautiful and Ruth was nothing remarkable; perhaps it was a question of colouring and complexion. Whatever the reason, everyone looked at Effie in a special way. Both sisters were fair with the fair-lashed look and faint eyebrows of some Dutch portraits.

It was Edward who introduced Effie to Harvey Gotham. Effie was in the habit of despising the rich, but she married him. They had a small house in Chelsea and at first they travelled everywhere together.

When Edward became an actor, Ruth got a job in a university, teaching twentieth century history. Edward had a television part which came to an end about the time Ruth discerned that Effie and Harvey were not getting on. Effie's young men-friends from her days of welfare-work were always in her house, discussing their social conscience. Harvey was often away.

"You're sleeping around," Ruth said to Effie.

"What do you mean?" she said.

"I know," Ruth said.

"What do you know?"

Ruth said, "I know all about it." What she meant was that she knew Effie.

"You must be guessing," said Effie, very shaken.

"I know," Ruth said, "that you're having affairs. Not one only. Plural."

Edward was still out of a job. They hadn't any prospect of a holiday that year, but Effie and Harvey had planned a motoring trip in Italy.

Ruth said, "Why don't you get Harvey to invite us to join you on your holiday in Italy?"

"He wouldn't like that," she said. "Four in the car."

"It's a big car."

"You couldn't afford your share," said Effie, "could you?"

"No, not all of it."

"What all this has to do with my love affairs, real or imagined," said Effie, "I really do not know."

"Don't you?" said Ruth.

"Ruth," she said, "you're a blackmailer, aren't you?"

"Only in your eyes. In my eyes it is simply that we're going to come to Italy with you. Harvey won't mind the money."

"Oh, God," she said, "I'd rather you went ahead and told him all you know. Think of all the suffering in the world, the starving multitudes. Can't you sacrifice a pleasure? Go ahead and tell Harvey what you know. Your sordid self-interest, your—"

"You shock me," Ruth said. "Stick to the point. Is it likely that I would go to your husband and say . . . ?"

They went on holiday with Effie and Harvey, and they took Ruth's student, Nathan, as well. Effie stole two bars of chocolate from the supermarket on the *autostrada* and Harvey left them abruptly. It was the end of their marriage. Fortunately Effie had enough money on her to pay for the rest of the trip. It was a holiday of great beauty. Effie tried to appreciate the pictures in the art galleries, the fountains in the squares, the ancient monuments and the Mediterranean abundance, but even basking on the beach she was uneasy.

Harvey saw Effie's features in Ruth; it struck him frequently that she was what Effie should have been. It had

48

been that situation where the visitor who came to stay remained to live. (Harvey had heard of an author who had reluctantly granted an interview to a young critic, who then remained with him for life.) The arrangement was not as uncomfortable as it might have been, for Ruth had claimed and cleared one of the shacks outside the house, where she spent most of the daytime with the baby. She was careful to make the changes unobtrusively. Delivery vans drove up with rugs or with an extra stove, but it was all done in a morning. Harvey paid for the things. When the baby cried it upset him, but that was seldom, for Ruth drove off frequently with the child, no doubt to let it cry elsewhere. She took it with her when she went shopping.

It was three weeks after she had arrived that Ruth said, "I'm going to write to Edward."

"I have written," said Harvey.

"I know," she said, and he wondered how she knew, since he had posted the letter himself. "But I'll write myself. I couldn't be the wife of an actor again."

"If he was a famous actor?"

"Well, he isn't a famous actor. A part here, a part there, and sometimes a film. So full of himself when he has a part. It was a much better life for me when he was a curate."

But she had no nostalgia even for those days of church fêtes, evening lectures and sewing classes. She already had a grip of her new life, dominated as it was by the Book of Job.

"You feel safer when you're living with someone who's in the God-business," Harvey said. "More at home."

"Perhaps that's it," she said.

"And a steadier income."

"Such as it is," she said, for she asked little for herself. "But," she said, "I was bored. He always agreed with me, and you don't."

"That's because you're one of my comforters," Harvey said. "Job had his comforters to contend with; why shouldn't I?"

"Do you think of yourself as Job?"

"Not exactly, but one can't help sympathizing with the man."

"I don't know about that," said Ruth. "Job was a very rich man. He lost all his goods, and all his sons and daughters, and took it all very philosophically. He said, 'The Lord gave, the Lord taketh away, blessed be the name of the Lord.' Then he gets covered with boils; and it's only then that his nerve gives way, he's touched personally. He starts his complaint against God at that point only. No question of why his sons should have lost their lives, no enquiries of God about the cause of their fate. It's his skin disease that sets him off."

"Maybe it was shingles," Harvey said. "A nervous disease. Anyway, it got on his nerves."

Ruth said, "He had to be touched himself before he would react. Touched in his own body. Utterly selfish. He doesn't seem to have suffered much or he wouldn't have been able to go into all that long argument. He couldn't have had a temperature."

"I don't agree. I think he had a high temperature all through the argument," Harvey said. "Because it's high poetry. Or else, maybe you're right; maybe it was the author who had the temperature. Job himself just sat there with a long face arguing against the theories of his friends."

"Make a note of that," Ruth commanded.

"I'll make a note." He did so.

"Someone must have fed him," said Ruth. "Someone must have brought him meals to eat as he sat on the dung-hill outside the town."

"I'm not sure he sat on a dung-hill outside the town. That is an assumption based on an unverified Greek version of the text. He is merely said to have sat in the ashes on the ground. Presumably at his own hearth. And his good wife, no doubt, brought him his meals."

Ruth had proved to be an excellent cook, cramped in the kitchen with that weird three-tiered kerosene stove of hers.

"What do you mean, 'his good wife,' " Ruth said. "She told him, 'Curse God and die.' "

"That was a way of expressing her exasperation. She was tired of his griping and she merely wanted him to get it off his chest quickly, and finish."

"I suppose the wife suffered," said Ruth. "But whoever wrote the book made nothing of her. Job deserved all he got."

"That was the point that his three friends tried to get across to him," Harvey said. "But Job made the point that he didn't deserve it. Suffering isn't in proportion to what the sufferer deserves."

Ruth wrote in September:

Dear Edward,

I suppose you have gathered by now that I've changed my mind about Harvey. I don't know what he's written to you.

He really is a most interesting man. I believe I can help Harvey.

I can't return to face the life we had together, ever again. My dear, I don't know how I could have thought I would. My plan was, as you know, entirely different. I feel Harvey needs me. I am playing a role in his life. He is serious. Don't imagine I'm living in luxury. He never mentions his wealth. But of course I am aware that if there is anything I require for myself or Clara, I can have it.

You may have heard from Ernie Howe that he is coming to visit Clara. She's well and pretty, and full of life.

I'm sure you have heard from Harvey how things are between him and me. It's too soon to talk of the future.

This has been a difficult letter to write. I know that you'll agree with what I say. You always do.

Ruth

She gave Harvey the letter to read, watching him while he read it. He looked younger than Edward, probably because of Edward's beard, although he was a little older. Harvey was lean and dark, tall, stringy.

"It's a bit dry," Harvey said.

"It's all I can do. Edward knows what I'm like."

"I suppose," said Harvey, "he'll be hurt."

"He doesn't love me," Ruth said.

"How do you know?"

"How does one know?"

"Still, he won't want to lose his property."

"That's something else."

Now, in October, Ruth was talking about sending to England for cretonne fabric. "One can't get exactly what I want in France," she said.

Harvey wrote,

Dear Edward,
    Thanks for yours.
    The infant is cutting a tooth and makes a din at night. Ruth has very disturbed nights. So do I. It's been raining steadily for three days. Ernie Howe came. We had a chat. He seems to feel fraternal towards me because we both had to do with Effie. He wants to talk about Effie. I don't. Afterwards, in the place next door that Ruth has fixed up for herself and Clara, Ernie asked her if she would go home and live with him and bring the baby. Ruth said no. I think he's after Ruth because she reminds him of Effie. He said he wouldn't take the child away from Ruth if she doesn't want to part with it, which she doesn't.
    I'm sorry to hear that you don't miss Ruth. You ought to.
    Cheque enclosed. I know you're not "selling your wife." Why should I think you are? You took money before I was sleeping with Ruth, so where's the difference?
    I don't agree the comforters just came to gloat. They relieved Job's suffering by arguing with him, keeping him talking. In different ways they keep insinuating that Job "deserved" his misfortunes; he must have done something wrong. While Job insists that he hasn't, that the massed calamities that came on him haven't any relation to his own actions. He

53

upsets all their theology. Those three friends of his are very patient and considerate, given their historical position. But Job is having a nervous crisis. He can't sleep. See 7:13–16.

> When I say, My bed shall comfort me, my couch shall ease my complaint;
>
> Then thou scarest me with dreams, and terrifiest me through visions:
>
> So that my soul chooseth strangling, and death rather than my life.
>
> I loathe it; I would not live alway: let me alone . . .

So I say, at least the three comforters kept him company. And they took turns as analyst. Job was like the patient on the couch.

Ruth doesn't sympathize with Job. She sees the male pig in him. That's a point of view.

The baby has started to squawk. I don't know what I'm going to do about the noise.

Yours,
Harvey

Ruth came in, jogging in her arms the baby Clara who had a whole fist in her mouth and who made noises of half-laughing, half-crying. Soon, she would start to bawl. Ruth's hair fell over her face, no longer like that of a curate's wife.

"Did you know that they want to sell the château?" she said.

The château was half a mile up the grassy pathway which led away from the cottage. Harvey knew the owner and had seen the house; that was when he first rented the cottage. He knew it was up for sale, and had been for some years.

"It's falling to bits," he said to Ruth.

"What a pity to neglect it like that!" Ruth said. "It's a charming house. It reminds me of something from my childhood, I don't know quite what. Perhaps somewhere we visited. I think something could be done to it."

She brought the fretful child close to Harvey so that he could make an ugly face. He showed his teeth and growled, whereupon Clara temporarily forgot her woes. She smelt of sour milk.

IV

Up at the château where the neglected lawns were greener than the patch round Harvey's house, and where the shrubberies were thick and very dark evergreen, the workmen were putting in the daylight hours of the last few days before the Christmas holidays. Ruth had already reclaimed one wing for habitation. The roof had been secured in that part, but most of the rooms were cold. She had arranged one sitting room, however, with a fire, and two bedrooms with oil stoves. A good start.

What a business it had been to persuade Harvey to buy the château! And now he was enchanted. Once he agreed to buy—and that was the uphill work—it was simple. Harvey sent for his London lawyer, Stewart Cowper, and for his French lawyer, Martin Deschamps, to meet in Nancy and discuss the deal with the family who owned the château. Ruth had gone with Harvey to this meeting, in October, with Clara in her folding pram. When the hotel room got too boring for the baby, Ruth hushed her, put her in her pram and took her for a walk in Place Stanislas. It was not long before Ruth saw through the splendid gilt gates the whole business group, with Harvey, trooping out to take the sun and continue the deal in the glittering square. Harvey and his two lawyers, the three members of the de Remiremont family, which comprised a middle-aged man, his daughter and his nephew, came and joined Ruth. The daughter put her hand on the handle of the pram. They all ambled round in a very unprofessional way, talking of notaries and tax and the laws governing foreigners' property in France. You could see that this was only a preliminary.

Harvey said, "We have to leave you. I'm writing a book on the *Book of Job*."

It was difficult to get across to them what the *Book of Job* was. Harvey's French wasn't at fault, it was their knowledge of the Bible, of which, like most good Catholics, they had scant knowledge. They stood around, the father in his old tweed coat and trousers, the daughter and nephew in their woollen jumpers and blue jeans, puzzling out what was *Job*. Finally, the father remembered. It all came back to him. "You shouldn't be in a hurry, then," he said. "Job had patience, isn't that right? One says, 'The patience of Job.' "

"In fact," said Harvey, "Job was the most impatient of men."

"Well, it's good to know what it is you're writing in that wretched little cottage," said the elder man. "I often wondered."

"I hope we'll soon have the house," said Ruth.

"So do we," said the owner. "We'll be glad to get rid of it." The young man and the girl laughed. The lawyers looked a little worried about the frankness and the freedom, suspecting, no doubt, some façade covering a cunning intention.

Ruth and Harvey left them then. It was all settled within a month except for the final bureaucracy, which might drag on for years. Anyhow, Harvey had paid, and Ruth was free to order her workmen to move in.

"Instead of disabusing myself of worldly goods in order to enter the spirit of *Job* I seem to acquire more, ever more and more," was all that Harvey said.

Ruth wrote to Effie with her letter-pad on her knee, beside the only fireplace, while the workmen hammered away, a few days before Christmas.

> Dear Effie,
>
> I really am in love with Harvey and you have no reason to say I am not. The lovely way he bought the house—so casual—we just walked round the *Place* with Clara and the family who used to own the château—and Harvey shook hands and that was all. The lawyers are working it out, but the house is ours.
>
> I can't make out your letter. You don't want Clara, at least not the bother of her. You despise Harvey. What do you mean, that I have stolen your husband and your child? Be civilized.

Ruth stopped, read what she had written, and tore it up. Why should I reply to Effie? What do I owe her? She stole a bit of chocolate, on principle. I stole her husband, not on principle. As for her child, I haven't stolen her, she has abandoned her baby. All right, Effie is young and beautiful, and now has to work for her living. Possibly she's broke.

> Dear Effie,
>   What attracted me most about the château was the woodpecker in the tree outside the bedroom window. Why don't you come and visit Clara?
>
>   Love,
>   Ruth

She sealed it up and put it on the big plate in the hall to be posted, for all the world as if the château was already a going concern. The big plate on a table by the door was all there was in the huge dusty hall, but it was a beginning.

Now she took sleeping Clara in her carry-cot and set her beside the driver's seat in the car. She put in a basket in the back, containing bread, pâté, a roast bantam hen and a bottle of Côte du Rhône, and set off down the drive to Harvey's house for lunch. The tired patch of withered shrubbery round Harvey's cottage was still noticeably different from the rest of the château's foliage, although Ruth had dug around a few bushes to improve them, and planted some bulbs. As soon as she pushed open the door she saw he had a visitor. She dumped the food basket and went back for the baby, having glimpsed the outline of a student, a young man, any student, with those blue jeans of such a tight fit, they were reminiscent of Elizabethan women's breasts, in that you wondered, looking at their portraits, where they put their natural flesh. The student followed her out to the car. It was

Nathan. "Nathan! It's you—you here. I didn't recognize
. . ." He woke Clara with his big kiss, and the child
wailed. He picked her up and pranced up and down with
the wakened child. Harvey's studious cottage was a car-
nival. Harvey said to Ruth, "I've told Nathan there will
be room for him up at the house."

Nathan had brought some food, too. He had been
skilful as ever in finding the glasses, the plates; everything was set for lunch. Ruth got Clara back to sleep
again, but precariously, clutching a ragged crust.

Harvey said very little. He had closed the notebook
he was working on, and unnaturally tidied his papers; his
pens were arranged neatly, and everything on his writing-table looked put-away. He sat looking at the floor
between his feet.

Nathan announced, "I just had to come. I had nothing else to do. It's a long time since I had a holiday."

"And Edward, how's Edward?" Ruth said.

"Don't you hear from Edward?"

"Yes of course," said Ruth, and Harvey said the same.

Nathan opened his big travel pack and brought out
yet more food purchases that he had picked up on the
way: cheese, wine, pâté and a bottle of Framboise. He
left the pack open while he took them to the table.
Inside was a muddle of clothes and spare shoes, but
Harvey noticed the edges of Christmas-wrapped parcels
sticking up from the bottom of the pack. My God, he
has come for Christmas. Harvey looked at Ruth: did she
invite him? Ruth fluttered about with her thanks and her
chatter.

"Are you off to Paris for Christmas?" Harvey enquired.
This was his first meeting with Nathan since the holiday
in Italy when Harvey had abandoned his party on the

autostrada; he felt he could be distant and impersonal without offence.

"I've come mainly to visit Clara for Christmas," said Nathan. He was lifting the baby out of the carry-cot.

"Let her sleep," Harvey said.

"Oh, Nathan must stay over Christmas," Ruth said. "Paris will be crowded. And dreadfully expensive." She added, "Nathan is a marvellous cook."

"So I have heard."

Ruth didn't notice, or affected not to notice, a look of empty desperation on Harvey's face; a pallor, a cornered look; his lips were parted, his eyes were focussing only on some anguished thought. And he was, in fact, suddenly aghast: What am I doing with these people around me? Who asked this fool to come and join us for Christmas? What do I need with Christmas, and Ruth, and a baby and a bloody little youth who needs a holiday? Why did I buy that château if not for Ruth and the baby to get out of my way? He looked at his writing-table, and panicked.

"I'm going out, I'll just fetch my coat," he said, thumping upstairs two at a time.

"Harvey, what's the matter?" said Ruth when he appeared again with his sheepskin jacket, his woollen hat. Rain had started to splash down with foul eagerness.

"Don't you want lunch?" she said.

"Excuse me. I'm studious," said Harvey, as he left the cottage. The car door slammed. The starter wouldn't work at first try. The sound of Harvey working and working at the starter became ever more furious until finally he was off.

When he came back in the evening the little house was deserted, all cleaned up. He poured himself a whisky, sat down and started to think of Effie. She was different from Ruth, almost a race apart. Ruth was kind, or comparatively so. Effie wasn't comparatively anything, certainly not kind. She was absolutely fascinating. Harvey remembered Effie at parties, her beauty, part of which was a quick-witted merriment. How could two sisters be so physically alike and yet so totally different? At any moment Ruth might come in and reproach him for not having the Christmas spirit. Effie would never do that. Ruth was thoroughly bourgeois by nature; Effie, anarchistic, aristocratic. I miss Effie, I miss her a lot, Harvey told himself. The sound of Ruth's little car coming down the drive, slowly in the mist, chimed with his thought as would the stroke of eight if there was a clock in the room. He looked at his watch; eight o'clock precisely. She had come to fetch him for dinner; three dinner-places set out on the table of the elegant room in the château, and the baby swinging in a hammock set up in a corner.

Ruth came in. "You know, Harvey," she said, "I think you might be nicer to Nathan. After all, it's Christmas time. He's come all this way, and one should have the Christmas spirit."

Nathan was there, at the château, settled in for Christmas. Harvey thought: I should have told him to go. I should have said I wanted Ruth and the baby to myself for Christmas. Why didn't I?—Because I don't want them to myself. I don't want them enough; not basically.

Ruth looked happy, having said her say. No need to say any more. I can't hold these women, Harvey thought. Neither Effie nor Ruth. My mind isn't on them enough, and they resent it, just as I resent it when they put something else before me, a person, an idea. Yes, it's understandable.

He swallowed down a drink and put on his coat.

"Nathan thinks it was marvellous of you to buy the château just to make me comfortable with Clara," said Ruth.

"I bought it for myself, too, you know. I always thought I might acquire it."

"Nathan has been reading the *Book of Job*, he has some ideas."

"He did his homework, you mean. He must think I'm some sort of monster. In return for hospitality he thinks he has to discuss my subject."

"He's polite. Besides, it's my subject too, now," said Ruth.

"Why?" said Harvey. "Because I've put you in the château?"

He thought, on the way through the misty trees that lined the long drive, They think I'm such a bore that I have to bribe them to come and play the part of comforters.

He made himself cheerful at the château; he poured drinks. In his anxiety to avoid the subject of *Job*, to be normal, to make general conversation, Harvey blurted out the other thing he had on his mind: "Any news of Effie?"

God, I've said the wrong thing. Both Nathan and Ruth looked, for a moment, startled, uncomfortable; both, discernibly, for different reasons. Nathan, Harvey supposed, had been told to avoid the subject of Effie. Ruth didn't want to bring Effie into focus; it was enough that she was still Harvey's wife, out there vaguely somewhere else, out of sight.

"Effie?" said Ruth.

"I heard from her," said Nathan. "Only a postcard, after she got out."

"Out from where?"

"From prison in Trieste. Didn't you hear about it?"

"Harvey never discusses Effie," said Ruth. "I've only just heard about it. She wrote to me last week from London, but she didn't mention prison."

"What happened?" said Harvey.

"She was caught shoplifting in a supermarket in Trieste. She said she did it to obtain an opportunity to study a women's prison at first-hand. She got out after three days. There was a small paragraph about it in the *Telegraph*, nothing in the other papers; it was about a month ago," Ruth said. "Nathan just told me."

"All she said on the card was that she was going to Munich," said Nathan.

"I wish her well of Munich," said Harvey.

"I thought it was a beautiful town," Ruth said.

"You thought strangely. There is a carillon clock with dancers coming out of the clock-tower twice a day. That's all there is in Munich."

"She has friends there," Nathan said. "She said on the card she was joining friends in Munich. She seems to be getting around."

"Well, I'm glad, for Effie, there is something else in Munich besides the carillon clock. Who made this soup?"

"Nathan did," said Ruth.

"It's great." He wondered why Stewart Cowper hadn't told him about Effie being arrested. He felt over-protected. How can you deal with the problem of suffering if everybody conspires to estrange you from suffering? He felt like the rich man in the parable: it is easier for a camel to go through the eye of a needle than for him to enter the Kingdom of Heaven.

"One must approach these things with balanced thought," Ruth was saying, alarmingly. Harvey bent his mind to take in what they were discussing. It emerged that they were talking about the huge price Nathan had paid for the taxi from the airport to the château.

"There's a train service," Harvey said.

"I've just been telling him that," said Ruth. "Spending all that money, as much as the air fare. He could have phoned me from the airport."

"I don't have the number," said Nathan.

"Oh, yes, I forgot," said Ruth. "No-one gets the number. Harvey has to be protected; in his position everyone wants him for something. He's here to study an important subject, write a thesis, get away from it all. You have to realize that, Nathan."

Nathan turned to Harvey. "Maybe I shouldn't have told you about Effie."

"Oh, that's all right. I asked you about her, after all."

"Yes, you did," said Ruth. She had served veal, delicately cooked in white wine. "You did bring up the subject, Harvey."

"A beautiful girl, Effie," said Nathan. "What a lovely girl she is!"

Harvey wondered how much he knew about how beautiful Effie was. He looked at Nathan and thought: He has barged into my peace, he's taking his place for Christmas, he's discussing my wife as if she was everybody's girl (which she is), and he's going to get together again with Ruth; they will conspire how to protect me. Finally, he will ask me for a loan.

"Will you be all right up here alone in the château tonight?" Harvey said with determination. "Ruth and I always shack down in my cottage; Ruth brings the baby back here immediately after early breakfast so that I can start on my work at about seven-thirty."

"If you'll leave Clara with me I won't feel lonely," said Nathan.

"Not at all," said Harvey. "We have a place for her. She's teething."

"Nathan's used to Clara," said Ruth. "He's known her and looked after her since she was born."

"I don't think we need ask our guests to baby-sit for us." Don't think, Harvey said within himself, that you are one of the family here; you are one of "our guests" in this house.

"Well, as she's teething," said Ruth, "I'd better take her with me. I really do think so, Nathan."

"We'll move up here to the château for Christmas," Harvey said, now that Ruth was winding up the feast with a cheese *soufflé* as light as could be. He fetched the brandy glasses.

V

Dear Edward,

Happy New Year. Thanks for yours.

The day before Christmas Eve he turned up. After dinner he sat up late discussing his ideas on *Job*—he'd done some reading (for my benefit, which I suppose is a compliment). I don't agree with you that he seems "positively calculating," I don't agree at all. I think he wanted to spend Christmas with Ruth and the baby. He would have preferred to spend Christmas with Effie. He didn't want to spend Christmas alone with you; that's why you're sour. You should get a lot of friends and some of your colleagues, pretty young actresses, have parties. Nathan would like that.

We went to Midnight Mass at the local church. Nathan carried Clara in a sling on his back and she slept throughout. There was a great crowd.

He hasn't left yet. He shows no sign of leaving.

I agree that Job endlessly discusses morals but there is nothing moral about the *Book of Job*. In fact it is shockingly amoral.

God has a wager with Satan that Job will not lose faith, however much he is afflicted. Job never knows about this wager, neither do his friends. But the reader knows. Satan finally makes the explicit challenge (2, 5)

> But put forth thy hand now, and touch his bone and his flesh, and he will curse thee to thy face.

And God says "Go ahead." ("Behold, he is in thine hand; but save his life.")

Consequently Job, having lost his sons and his goods, is now covered with sores. He is visited by his bureaucratic friends who tell him he must have deserved it. The result is that Job has a sort of nervous breakdown. He demands an explanation and he never gets it.

Do you know that verse of Kipling's—?

> The toad beneath the harrow knows
> Exactly where each tooth-point goes;
> The butterfly upon the road
> Preaches contentment to that toad.

I think this expresses Job's plight. The boils are personal, they loosen his tongue, they set him off. He doesn't reproach God in so many words, but he does by implication.

I must tell you that early in the New Year we started to be bothered by people hanging around the house. Some "tourists" (at this time of year!) went to the château and asked if they could see round the house—a couple of young men. Nathan got rid of them. Ruth says she heard there were "strangers" in the village shop asking questions about me the other day. A suspicious-looking workman came to my cottage, saying he'd been sent to test the electricity (not to read the meter, but to test). He showed me his card, it looked all right. But the electricity department hadn't heard of him. We suspect that Effie is putting in some private detectives. I've written to Stewart Cowper. Where would she get the money?

Why didn't you tell me that Effie had been arrested for shoplifting in Trieste?

I hope you get that part in the play you write about in your letter. You must know by now.

Yours,
Harvey

Please check the crocodiles for me at the London Zoo. Their eyelids are vertical, are they not? Leviathan in *Job* is generally supposed to be the crocodile. It is written of Leviathan "his eyes are like the eyelids of the morning." None of the commentaries is as yet satisfactory on this. You may remember they never were.

PART II

VI

THE VILLAGE SHOP, about two kilometres from Harvey's cottage, was normally busy when, about nine in the morning, Harvey stopped to buy a newspaper and cigarettes. He remembered this clearly later, when the day had developed and in the later profusion of events he set about to decipher them, starting from this, the beginning of his day.

The shop was divided into two parts, one leading into the other. The owner, a large man in his forties, wearing a dark grey working apron the colour of his hair, looked after the part which sold groceries, detergents, ham, pâté, sausage, cheese, fruit, vegetables, all well laid-out; and also a large stock of very good Vosges wines stacked in rows and arranged according to types and prices. The other part of the shop was presided over by the wife, plump, ruddy-cheeked, with short black curly hair, in her mid-thirties. She looked after the coffee machine, the liquor bar, the pre-wrapped buns and sweets, the newspapers and cigarettes, some stationery and other conveniently saleable goods.

That morning Harvey took an espresso coffee, his packet of cigarettes and the Vosges local paper which he scarcely glanced at. He looked around as he drank his coffee; the suspect people were not there to-day; it was not to be expected that they would always be at the bar, it would have been too obvious had they been hanging around all day and every day: two young Belgians, touring forests and caves, students, campers, the shopkeepers had said. It seemed unlikely; they were too old for students. There had been another man and woman, older still, in their forties; they looked like a couple of *concièrges* from Paris. Harvey was convinced these were Effie's detectives, getting enough evidence for Effie's huge alimonial scoop. The owners of the shop had seemed to take them for granted as they walked up and down the road. The so-called Belgians had a camper with a Lyons registration number—that meant nothing, they had probably hired it. The middle-aged couple, both of them large and solid, came and went in a sad green Citroën Dyane 6. Harvey, having got such a brisk reply to his casual enquiries about the Belgians, had not ventured to enquire about the second couple. Maybe the shopkeepers were in their pay.

This morning, the strangers were not in sight. Only two local youths were at the bar; some countrywomen queued up at the counter on the grocery side. Harvey drank his coffee, paid, took up his paper and cigarettes and left. As he went out he heard behind him the chatter of the women, just a little more excited and scandalized than usual. *"Les supermarchés, les supermarchés . . ."* was the phrase he took in most, and assumed there was a discussion in progress about prices and food.

He put down the paper beside him and as he drove off his eye caught a picture on the front page. It was a group of three identikits, wanted people, two men and a girl. The outlines of the girl's face struck him as being rather like Ruth's. He must remember to let her see it. He turned at the end of the road towards Epinal, the town he was bound for.

After about two kilometres he ran into a road-block; two police motor-cycles, three police cars, quite a lot. It was probably to do with the identikits. Harvey produced his papers and sat patiently while the policeman studied them, gave a glance at the car, and waved him on. While waiting, Harvey looked again at the newspaper on the seat by his side. The feature with the identikits was headed "Armed Robberies in the Vosges." Undoubtedly the police were looking for the gang. At Epinal he noticed a lot of police activity outside the commissariat on the banks of the Moselle, and above that at the grand prefecture. There, among the fountains and flags, he could see in the distance flashes of blue and white uniforms, blue, red and white police cars, a considerable display. He noticed, and yet took no notice. He had come to look once more, as he had often done before, at the sublime painting, *Job Visited by His Wife* at the Musée of Epinal. He parked his car and went in.

He was well known to the receptionist, who gave him a sunny greeting as he passed the desk.

"No schoolchildren to-day," she said. Sometimes when there were school-groups or art-college students in the gallery Harvey would turn away, not even attempting to see the picture. But very often there were only one or two visitors. Sometimes, he had the museum to himself; he was already half-way up the stairs when the receptionist told him so; she watched him approvingly, even admiringly, as he ran up the staircase, as if even his long legs, when they reached the first turning of the stairs, had brought a touch of pleasure into her morning. The dark-blue custodian with his hands behind his back as he made his stately round, nodded familiarly as Harvey reached the second floor; as usual the man went to sit patiently on a chair at the other end of the room as Harvey took his usual place on a small bench in front of the picture.

The painting was made in the first part of the seventeenth century by Georges de La Tour, a native of Lorraine. It bears a resemblance to the Dutch candlelight pictures of the time. Its colours and organization are superb. It is extremely simple, and like so much great art of the past, surprisingly modern.

Job visité par sa femme: To Harvey's mind there was much more in the painting to illuminate the subject of Job than in many of the lengthy commentaries that he knew so well. It was eloquent of a new idea, and yet, where had the painter found justification for his treatment of the subject?

Job's wife, tall, sweet-faced, with the intimation of a beautiful body inside the large tent-like case of her firm clothes, bending, long-necked, solicitous over Job. In her hand is a lighted candle. It is night, it is winter; Job's wife wears a glorious red tunic over her dress. Job sits on a plain cube-shaped block. He might be in front of a fire, for the light of the candle alone cannot explain the amount of light that is cast on the two figures. Job is

naked except for a loin cloth. He clasps his hands above
his knees. His body seems to shrink, but it is the shrunk-
enness of pathos rather than want. Beside him is the
piece of broken pottery that he has taken to scrape his
wounds. His beard is thick. He is not an old man. Both
are in their early prime, a couple in their thirties. (Indeed, their recently dead children were not yet married.)
His face looks up at his wife, sensitive, imploring some
favour, urging some cause. What is his wife trying to tell
him as she bends her sweet face towards him? What does
he beg, this stricken man, so serene in his faith, so
accomplished in argument?

The scene here seemed to Harvey so altogether different from that suggested by the text of *Job*, and yet so
deliberately and intelligently contemplated that it was
impossible not to wonder what the artist actually meant.
Harvey stared at the picture and recalled the verses that
followed the account of Job's affliction with boils.

> *And he took him a potsherd to scrape himself withal;
> and he sat down among the ashes.*
> *Then said his wife unto him, Dost thou still retain
> thine integrity? curse God, and die.*
> *But he said unto her, Thou speakest as one of the
> foolish women speaketh. What? shall we receive good at
> the hand of God, and shall we not receive evil? In all
> this did not Job sin with his lips.*

But what is she saying to him, Job's wife, in the serious, simple and tender portrait of Georges de La Tour?
The text of the poem is full of impatience, anger; it is as
if she is possessed by Satan. "Dost thou still retain thine
integrity?" She seems to gloat, "curse God and die."

77

Harvey recalled that one of the standard commentators has suggested a special interpretation, something to the effect, "Are you still going to be so righteous? If you're going to die, curse God and get it off your chest first. It will do you good." But even this, perhaps homely, advice doesn't fit in with the painting. Of course, the painter was idealizing some notion of his own; in his dream, Job and his wife are deeply in love.

Some people had just arrived in the museum; Harvey could hear voices downstairs and footsteps mounting. He continued to regard the picture, developing his thoughts: Here, she is by no means the carrier of Satan's message. She comes to comfort Job, reduced as he is to a mental and physical wreck. "You speak," he tells her, "as one of the foolish women;" that is to say, he doesn't call her a foolish woman, he rather implies that she isn't speaking as her normal self. And he puts it to her, "Shall we receive good at the hand of God, and shall we not receive evil?" That domestic "we" is worth noticing, thought Harvey; he doesn't mean to abandon his wife, he has none of the hostility towards her that he has, later, for his friends. In order to have a better look at Job's wife's face, Harvey put his head to one side. Right from the first he had been struck by her resemblance to Effie in profile. She was like Ruth, too, but more like Effie, especially about the upper part of her face. Oh, Effie, Effie, Effie.

There were people behind Harvey. He glanced round and was amazed to see four men facing towards him, not looking at the other pictures as he had expected. Nor were they looking at the painting of Job. They were looking at him, approaching him. At the top of the staircase two other men in police uniform appeared. The keeper looked embarrassed, bewildered. Harvey got up to face them. He realized that, unconsciously, he had been hearing police sirens for some time. With the picture of Job still in his mind's eye, Harvey had time only to form an abrupt impression before they moved in on him, frisked him, and invited him to descend to the waiting police cars.

Harvey had time to go over again all the details of the morning later, in between interrogations. He found it difficult to get the rest of his life into focus; everything seemed to turn on the morning: the time he had stopped at the village shop; the drive to Epinal; the thoughts that had gone through his mind in front of the painting, *Job visité par sa femme,* at the museum; the moment he was taken to the police car, and driven over the bridge to the commissariat for questioning.

He answered the questions with lucidity so long as they lasted. On and off, he was interrogated for the rest of the day and half the night.

"No, I've never heard of the FLE."

"*Front de la Libération de l'Europe.* You haven't heard of it?"

"No, I haven't heard of it."

"You know that your wife belongs to this organization?"

"I don't know anything about it."

"There was an armed robbery in a supermarket outside Epinal this morning. You were waiting here to join your wife."

"I'm separated from my wife. I haven't seen her for nearly two years."

"It was a coincidence that you were in Epinal this morning visiting a museum while your estranged wife was also in Epinal engaged in armed robbery?"

"If my wife was in Epinal, yes, it was a coincidence."

"Is that your English sense of humour?"

"I'm a Canadian."

"Is it a coincidence that other supermarkets and a jeweller's shop in the Vosges have been robbed by this gang in the last two weeks? Gérardmer, La Bresse, Baccarat; this morning, Epinal."

"I don't read the papers."

"You bought one this morning."

"I give no weight to local crimes." If Effie's involved, thought Harvey, plainly she's in this district to embarrass me. It was essential that he shouldn't suggest this, for at the same time it would point to Effie's having directive authority over the gang.

"I still can't believe that my wife's involved," said Harvey. He partly meant it.

"Three of them, perhaps four. Where are they?"

"I don't know. You'd better look."

"You recently bought the château. Why?"

"I thought I might as well. It was convenient."

"You've been a year at the cottage?"

"About a year and a half."

"How did you find it?"

"I've already explained—"

"Explain again."

"I found the cottage," recited Harvey, "because I was in the Vosges at that time. I had come here to Epinal expressly to look at the painting *Job Visited by His Wife* by Georges de La Tour. I had heard through some friends that the château was for sale. I went to look it over. I said I'd think about it, but I was struck by the suitability of the cottage to my needs, and took that on in the meantime. The owner, Claude de Remiremont, let me have it."

"How much rent do you pay?"

"I have no idea," Harvey said. "Very little. My lawyer attends to that."

(The rich!)

This interrogator was a man of about Harvey's age, not more than forty, black hair, blue eyes, a good strong face, tall. A chief inspector, special branch; no fool. His tone of voice varied. Sometimes he put his questions with the frank lilt of a query at the end; at other times he simply made a statement as if enunciating a proved fact. At the end of the table where they sat facing each other was a hefty policeman in uniform, older, with sandy hair growing thin and faded. The door of the room opened occasionally, and other men in uniform and ordinary clothes came and went.

"Where did you learn French?"

"I have always spoken French."

"You have taken part in the French-Canadian liberation movement."

"No."

"You don't believe in it?"

"I don't know anything about it," said Harvey. "I haven't lived in Canada since I was eighteen."

"You say that your wife's sister has been living with you since last October."

"That's right."

"With a baby."

"Yes. My wife's baby daughter."

"But there was a woman with a baby in your house for a year before that."

"Not at all. The baby was only born at the end of June last year."

"There was another infant in your house. We have evidence, M. Gotham, that there was a small child's washing on the line outside your house at least from April of last year."

"That is so. But there wasn't any baby, there wasn't any woman."

"Look, M. Gotham, it is a simple trick for terrorists to take the precaution, in the case of discovery, to keep a woman and a child in the house in order to avoid a shoot-out. Rather a low and dangerous trick, using a baby as a cover, but people of that nature—"

"There was no baby at all in my house, nobody but myself," Harvey explained patiently. "It was a joke—for the benefit of my brother-in-law who came to visit me. I brought some baby clothes and put them out on the line. He obviously thought I had a girl living with me. I only put them out a few times after that. I told my brother-in-law that I did it to keep women from bothering me with offers of domestic care. As they do. They would assume, you see, that there was a woman. I suppose I'm an eccentric. It was a gesture."

"A gesture."

"Well, you might say," said Harvey, thinking fast how to say it, "that it was a surrealistic gesture."

The inspector looked at Harvey for rather a long time. Then he left the room and came back with a photograph in his hand. Effie, in half-profile, three years ago, with her hair blowing around.

"Is that your wife?"

"Yes," said Harvey. "Where did you get this photograph?"

"And the woman you are living with, Ruth, is her sister?"

"Mme. Jansen is her sister. Where did you get this photograph of my wife? Have you been ransacking through my papers?"

The inspector took up the photograph and looked at it. "She resembles her sister," he said.

"Did you have a search warrant?" said Harvey.

"You will be free to contact a lawyer as soon as you have answered our questions. I presume you have a lawyer in Paris? He will explain the law to you."

"I have, of course, a French lawyer," Harvey said. "But I don't need him at the moment. Waste of money."

Just then a thought struck him: Oh, God, will they shoot Ruth in mistake for Effie?

"My sister-in-law, Ruth Jansen, is, as you say, very like her sister. She's caring for the baby of nine months. Be very careful not to confuse them should you come to a confrontation. She has the baby there in the château."

"We have the baby."

"What?"

"We are taking care of the baby."

"Where is she?"

The sandy-haired policeman spoke up. He had a perfectly human smile: "I believe she is taking the air in the courtyard. Come and see out of the window."

Down in the courtyard among the police cars and motor-bicycles, a large policeman in uniform, but without his hat, whom Harvey recognized as one of those who had escorted him from the museum, was holding Clara in his arms, wrapped up in her woollies; he was jogging her up and down while a young policewoman was talking to her. Another, younger policeman, in civilian clothes, was also attempting to curry favour with her. Clara had her chubby arms round the large man's neck, enjoying the attention, fraternizing with the police all round.

"Is she getting her feeds?" said Harvey. "I believe she has some special regular feeds that have to be—"

"Mme. Jansen is seeing to all that, don't worry. Let's proceed."

"I want to know where Ruth Jansen is," said Harvey.

"She's downstairs, answering some questions. The sooner we proceed with the job the sooner you will be able to join her. Why did you explain your baby clothes to your brother-in-law Edward Jansen in the words, 'The police won't shoot if there's a baby in the house'?"

"Did I say that?" said Harvey.

"Mme. Jansen has admitted it," said the inspector.

Admitted it. What had Edward told Ruth, what was Ruth telling them downstairs? But "admitted" was not the same as "volunteered" the information.

"You probably suggested the phrase to her," said Harvey. The old police trick: Is it true that he said "The police won't shoot . . . ?"

"Did you or did you not say those words last April when M. Jansen came to see you?"

"If I did it was a joke."

"Surrealism?"

"Yes, call it that."

"You are a man of means?"

"Oh, yes."

"Somebody is financing the FLE," said the inspector.

"But I am not financing it."

"Why do you live in that shack?"

"It doesn't matter to me where I work. I've told you. All I want is peace of mind. I'm studious."

"Scholarly," said the inspector dreamily.

"No, studious. I can afford to study and speculate without achieving results."

The inspector raised his shoulders and exchanged a glance with the sandy-haired policeman. Then he said, "Studious, scholarly . . . Why did you buy the château?"

"It was convenient for me to do so. Mme. Jansen thought it desirable for her to have a home for herself and the baby."

"It isn't your child."

It was Harvey's turn to shrug. "It's my wife's child. It makes no difference to me who the father is."

"The resemblance between your wife and her sister might be very convenient," said the inspector.

"I find them quite distinct. The resemblance is superficial. What do you mean—'convenient'?" Harvey, not quite knowing what the man was getting at, assumed he was implying that an exchange of lovers would be easy for him, the two sisters being, as it were, interchangeable. "They are very different," said Harvey.

"It would be convenient," said the inspector, "for two women who resemble each other to be involved in the same criminal organization. I am just hypothesizing, you understand. A question of one being able to provide an alibi for the other; it's not unknown . . . ."

"My papers are in order," Harvey said now, for no reason that was apparent, even to himself.

The inspector was very polite. "You maintain your wife financially, of course."

"I've given her no money since I left her. But if I had, that wouldn't signify that I was financing a terrorist organization."

"Then you know that your wife is an active member of the FLE, and consequently have refused to supply money."

"I never knew of the existence of the FLE until now. I don't at all know that my wife is a member of the group."

"And you give your wife no money," the policeman said.

"No money."

"You knew that she was arrested in Trieste."

"I didn't know until the other day. Nobody told me."

"Nobody told you," stated the inspector.

"That's right. Nobody told me. I'm studious, you see. I have arranged for people not to bother me, and they don't; rather to excess. I think someone should have told me. Not that it would have made any difference."

"Your wife knows where you live?"

"Yes."

"You have written to her?"

"No. I left her two years ago. Eventually she found out where I lived."

"How did she find out?"

"I suppose she got it out of someone. She's an intelligent woman. I doubt very much she's mixed up with a terrorist group."

"You must have had some reason to abandon her. Why are you so eager to protect her?"

"Look, I just want to be fair, to answer your questions."

"We know she's an activist in the FLE."

"Well, what exactly have they done?"

"Armed robbery and insurrection in various places. Of recent weeks they've been operating in the Vosges. Where are their headquarters?"

"Not in my house. And if my wife is involved in these incidents—which I don't admit she is—isn't it possible she has been kidnapped and forced to join this FLE? It's happened before. The Hearst case in the United States . . ."

"Do you have reason to believe she has been kidnapped?"

"I don't know. I have no idea. Has anyone been killed, injured, by this group?"

"Injured? But they are armed. They've collected a good deal of money, wounded twelve, damaged many millions of francs' worth of property. They are dangerous. Three men and a girl. The girl is your wife. Who are the others?"

"How should I know? I've never heard of the—"

"Nobody told you."

"Correct."

"It's time for lunch," said the inspector, looking at his watch; and, as he got up, he said, "Can you explain why Nathan Fox disappeared from the château last night?"

"Nathan Fox. Disappeared?"

"Nobody told you."

"No. I left my cottage at nine this morning."

"Where is Nathan Fox?" said the inspector, still standing.

"I have no idea. He's free to come and go . . . I don't really know."

"Well, think it over." The inspector left the room.

Harvey's cottage was in darkness when he drove back at four in the morning. He was tempted to go in and see what had happened to his papers, his work; had they been careful or had they turned everything upside down? Later, he found everything more or less intact with hardly a sign of a search; he had suspected that at least half the time he was kept for questioning had been for the purpose of giving the police leisure to continue their search at the cottage and the château; much good it had done them.

He didn't stop at the cottage that early morning, but drove up to the château. A police car was parked at a bend in the drive. Harvey tooted twice, softly and quickly, as he passed it. Friendly gesture. The light was on in the porch. He let himself in. Ruth came out of the living room in her dressing gown; she had been sleeping on a sofa, waiting for him. "They brought us back at half-past six," she said. She came to hug him, to kiss him. "Are you all right?" they both said at the same time. Clara was sleeping in her carry-cot.

The first thing that struck him was the colour in the room. There was nothing new, but after the grey and neutral offices, hour after hour, at the police headquarters, the blue of Ruth's dressing gown, the flower-patterned yellow sofa, green foliage arranged in a vase, the bright red tartan rug folded over Clara's cot, made a special impact on his senses. He smiled, almost laughed.

"Do you want to go to bed? Aren't you tired?" Ruth said.

"No. I'm wide awake."

"Me, too."

They poured whiskies and sodas. "I simply told them the truth," Ruth said. She decided she couldn't face her whiskey and took orange juice.

"Me, too. What else could one say?"

"Oh, I know you told them everything," Ruth said, "I could guess by the questions."

Harvey quoted, " 'The police won't shoot if there's a baby in the house.' "

"Yes, why did you bring that up?" said Ruth. "Was it necessary? They're suspicious enough—"

"I didn't suggest it to them."

"Well, neither did I," said Ruth. "The inspector asked me if it was true you'd made that remark. I said I believed so. Edward told me, of course—"

"They're quite clever," Harvey said. "How did they treat you?"

"Very polite. They were patient about my *au pair* French."

"How many?"

"Two plain-clothes men and a glamorous police-woman. Did you see the policewoman?" said Ruth.

"I saw one, from the window, playing with Clara."

"They were very decent about Clara."

Harvey's interrogators had been three, one after the other, then starting in the late afternoon with the first again.

Ruth and Harvey described and identified their respective policemen, and in a euphoric way compared a great many of their experiences of the day, questions and answers. Finally Ruth said, "Do you really think Effie's in it?"

"Up to the neck," said Harvey.

"Can you blame them for suspecting us?"

"No. I think, in fact, that Effie has chosen this district specifically to embarrass me."

"So do I."

He sat on the sofa beside her, relaxed, with his arm round her. She said, "You know, I'm more afraid of Effie than the police."

"Did you tell them that?"

"No."

"Did they come and look round the château while you were at the headquarters?"

"I don't think so, because when they brought me back they asked if they might have a look round. I said, of course. They went all over, attics, cellars, and both towers. Actually, I was quite relieved that they didn't find anything, or rather anyone. It would be easy to hide in this house, you know."

"Did you tell them you were relieved?"

"No."

"Now tell me about Nathan."

"It's a long story," said Ruth. "He's in love with Effie. He'd do anything she asked him." Her voice had changed to a mumble.

Harvey said, "But when did you know——" Then he stopped. "My God," he said, "I'm becoming another interrogator. I expect you've had enough."

"Quite enough."

It was he who had the idea to go and make breakfast, which he brought in on a tray. "I had a lousy pizza for supper," he said.

She said, "Nathan must have left last night. He didn't sleep here. He wasn't here when I came up from the cottage this morning. His bed wasn't slept in."

"Did Anne-Marie see him?" Anne-Marie was a local woman who had been coming daily to help in the house for the past two weeks.

"No, he wasn't here when she arrived at eight. He'd taken nothing special that I could see. But he had a phone call yesterday. He said it was from London. I was annoyed at the time, because I'd told him not to give anyone your number."

The telephone at the château operated through an exchange for long distance. "One could easily find out if it came from London," Harvey said.

"The police say there was no call from London," Ruth said.

"Then it might have been a national call. He could have been in touch with Effie."

"Exactly," she said.

"How much did you tell them about Nathan?"

"Everything I know."

"Quite right."

"And another thing," Ruth said, "I told them—"

"Let's forget it and go to bed."

Clara woke up just then. They shoved a piece of toast into her hand, which seemed to please her mightily.

It was nine-fifteen when the telephone rang. This time it was from London. At the same time the doorbell rang. Harvey had been dreaming that his interrogator was one of those electric typewriters where the typeface can be changed by easy manipulation; the voice of the interrogator changed like the type, and in fact, was one and the same, now roman, now élite, now italics. In the end, bells on the typewriter rang to wake him up to the phone and the doorbell.

He looked out of the window while Ruth went to answer the phone. Reporters, at least eight, some with cameras, some with open umbrellas or raincoats over their heads to shield them from the pouring rain. Up the drive came a television van. Behind him, through the door of the room, Ruth called to him, "Harvey, it's urgent for you, from London."

"Get dressed," Harvey said. "Don't open the door. Those are reporters out there. Keep them in the rain for a while, at least."

Clara began to wail. The doorbell pealed on. From round the side of the château someone was banging at another door.

On the phone was Stewart Cowper from London.

"What's going on there?" said Stewart.

Harvey thought he meant the noise.

"There's been a bit of trouble. Reporters are at the doors of the house and the baby's crying."

"There are headlines in all the English papers. Are you coming back to England?"

"Not at the moment," Harvey said. "I don't know about Ruth and the child; but we haven't discussed it. What are the headlines?"

"Headlines and paras, Harvey. Hold on, I'll read you a bit:

Millionaire's religious sect possibly involved in French terrorist activities. Wife of English actor involved . . .

And here's another,

Playboy Harvey Gotham, 35, with his arsenal of
money from Gotham's Canadian Salmon, whose
uncles made a fortune in the years before and during
the second world war, has been questioned by the
gendarmes d'enquêtes of the Vosges, France, in connection with hold-ups and bombings of supermarkets and post offices in that area. It is believed that
his wife, Mrs. Effie Gotham, 25, is a leading member of FLE, an extreme leftist terrorist movement.
Mr. Gotham, who has recently acquired a base in
that area, denies having in any way financed the
group or having been in touch with his estranged
wife. He claims to be occupied with religious studies. Among his circle are his sister-in-law, Ruth,
28, sister of the suspected terrorist, and Nathan
Fox, 25, who disappeared from the Gotham château
on the eve of the latest armed robbery at Epinal,
capital of the Vosges.

There's a lot more," said Stewart. "If you're not coming
back to England I'd better come there. Have you got
hold of Martin Deschamps?"

"Who the hell is he?"

"Your Paris lawyer."

"Oh, him. No. I don't need lawyers. I'm not a criminal. Look, I've got to get rid of these reporters. By the
way," Harvey continued, partly for the benefit of the
police who had undoubtedly tapped the phone, and
partly because he meant it, "I must tell you that the
more I look at La Tour's *Job* the more I'm impressed by

the simplicity, the lack of sentimentality above all. It's a magnificent—"

"Don't get on the wrong side of the press," shouted Stewart.

"Oh I don't intend to see them. Ruth and I have had very little sleep."

"Make an appointment for a press conference, late afternoon, say five o'clock," said Stewart. "I'll send you Deschamps."

"No need," said Harvey, and hung up.

Nonetheless, he managed to mollify the soaking press-men outside his house, speaking to them from an upstairs window, by making an appointment with them for five o'clock that afternoon. They didn't all go away, but they stopped battering at the doors.

Then, to Ruth's amazement their newly engaged, brisk domestic help, Anne-Marie, arrived, with a bag of pro-visions. It was her second week on the job. She managed to throw off the reporters who crowded round her with questions, by upbraiding them for disturbing the baby, and by pushing her way through. Inside the front door, Harvey stood ready to open it quickly, admitting her and nobody else.

"The police," Anne-Marie said, "were at my house yesterday for hours. Questions, questions." But she seemed remarkably cheerful about the questions.

VII

A LONG RING at the front
doorbell. Outside in the pouring rain a police car waited.
From the upper window Harvey saw the interrogator he
had left less than twelve hours ago in the headquarters
at Epinal.

"Ah," said Harvey from the window. "I've been missing you dreadfully."

"Look," said the man, "I'm not enjoying this, am I?
Just one or two small questions to clarify—"

"I'll let you in."

The policeman glanced through the open door at the
living room as he passed. Harvey conducted him to a
small room at the back of this part of the château. The
room had a desk and a few chairs; it hadn't been fur-
nished or re-painted; it was less smart and new than the
police station at Epinal, but it was the next best thing.

"You have no clue, absolutely no idea where your wife is?"

"No. Where do you yourselves think she is?"

"Hiding out in the woods. Or gone across into Germany. Or hiding in Paris. These people have an organization," said the inspector.

"If she's in the woods she would be wet," said Harvey, glaring at the sheet rain outside the window.

"Is she a strong woman? Any health complications?"

"Well, she's slim, rather fragile. Her health's all right so far as I know," Harvey said.

"If she contacts you, it would be obliging if you would invite her to the house. The same applies to Nathan Fox."

"But I don't want my wife in the house. I don't want to oblige her. I don't need Nathan Fox," Harvey said.

"When things quieten down she might try to contact you. You might oblige us by offering her a refuge."

"I should have thought you had the house surrounded."

"We do. We mean to keep it surrounded. You know, these people are heavily armed, they have sophisticated weapons. It might occur to them to take you hostages, you and the baby. Of course, they would be caught before they could get near you. But you might help us by issuing an invitation."

"It's all a supposition," Harvey said. "I'm not convinced that this woman-terrorist is my wife, nor that my wife is a terrorist. As for Nathan Fox, he's a mystery to me, but I wouldn't have thought he'd draw attention to himself by going off and joining an armed band at the very moment when they were active."

"If your wife is a fascinating woman—"

"I hope," said Harvey, "that you're taking special precautions to protect the baby."

"You admit that the baby might be in danger?"

"With an armed gang around, any baby might be in danger."

"But you admit that your wife's baby might be an object of special interest to your wife."

"She has taken no interest in the child."

"Then why are you suggesting that we specially protect this child?"

"I hope you have made arrangements to do so," said Harvey.

"We have your house and grounds surrounded."

"The baby," said Harvey, "must be sent back to England. My sister-in-law will take her."

"A good idea. We can arrange for them to leave, quietly, with every protection. But it would be advisable for you to keep the move as secret as possible. I mean the press. We don't want this gang to know every move. I warn you to be careful what you say to the press. The examining magistrate—"

"The press! They've already—"

The man spread his hands helplessly. "This wasn't my fault. These things leak out. After all, it's a matter of national concern. But not a word about your plans to send the child away."

"The maid will know. They talk—"

"Anne-Marie is one of our people," said the inspector.

"You don't say! We rather liked her."

"She'd better stay on with you, then. And hang out baby clothes on the line, as you always want to do. I might look in again soon."

"Don't stand on ceremony."

"How is it possible," Ruth said, "that the police think the gang might turn up here, now that this story's all over the papers, on the radio, the television? It's the last place they would come to. Clara's safer here than anywhere. How can they think—"

"The police don't think so, they only say they think so."

"Why?"

"How do I know? They suspect me strongly. They want the baby out of France. Maybe it's got something to do with their public image."

"I don't want to go," said Ruth.

"I don't want you to go," said Harvey, "but I think you should. It's only for a while. I think you must."

"Are you free to come, too? Harvey, let's both get away."

"On paper, I'm free to go. In fact, they might detain me. The truth is, I don't want to leave just at this moment. Just bloody-mindedness on my part."

"I can be stubborn, too," said Ruth; but she spoke with a fluidity that implied she was giving way. "But, after all," she went on, "I suppose you didn't ask me to come here in the first place."

Harvey thought, I don't love her, I'm not in the least in love with her. Much of the time I don't even like her very much.

Anne-Marie had put some soup on the table. Harvey and Ruth were silent before her, now that she wasn't a maid but a police auxiliary. When she had left, Ruth said, "I don't know if I'll be able to keep this down. I'm pregnant."

"How did that happen?" Harvey said.

"The same as it always happens."

"How long have you known?"

"Three weeks."

"Nobody tells me anything," Harvey said.

"You don't want to know anything."

Had Ruth stopped taking the pill? Was it his child or Nathan's? She didn't guess his first thought, but she did his second. "I never slept with Nathan, ever," she said. "His mind's on Effie—that's one thing I didn't mention to the police."

"Take some bread with your soup. You'll keep it down better."

"You know, I'd rather not go back to England. Now that Edward's having this amazing success—"

"What success?"

"He's having an astonishing success in the West End. That play—"

"Well, how long have you known about this?"

"Three weeks. It's been in the papers, and he wrote—"

"Nobody tells me anything."

"I think it funny Edward hasn't rung us up to-day. He must have seen the papers," Ruth said. "Maybe it scared him. A scandal."

"Where would you like to go?" Harvey said.

"Have you got anyone in Canada I could take Clara to?"

"I have an aunt and I have an uncle in Toronto. They're married but they live in separate houses. You could go to either. I'll ring up."

"I'll go to the uncle," said Ruth. She started to smile happily, but she was crying at the same time.

"There's nothing to worry about," Harvey said.

"Yes there is. There's Effie. There's Edward."

"What about Edward?"

"He's a shit. He might have wanted to know if I was all right. He's been writing all the time I've been here, and phoning every day since we got the telephone put in. Up to now."

Anne-Marie came in with a splendid salad, a tray of cheeses.

"Shall I help Madame to pack after lunch?" she said.

"How did she know I was leaving?" Ruth said when the maid had gone out.

"Somebody told her. Everyone knows everything," said Harvey, "except me."

Ruth was in the bedroom, packing, and Harvey was pushing the furniture here and there to make a distance between the place where he intended to sit to receive the reporters, and the part of the room reserved for them. Ruth, Harvey thought as he did so, has been crying a lot over the past few weeks, crying and laughing. I noticed, but I didn't notice. I wonder if she cried under the interrogation, and laughed? Anyway, it isn't this quite unlooked-for event that's caused her to cry and laugh, it started earlier. Did she tell the police she was pregnant? Probably. Maybe that's why they want to get rid of her. Is she really pregnant? Harvey plumped up a few cushions. Yellow chintzes, lots of yellow; at least, the chintzes had a basis of yellow, so that you saw yellow when you came into the room. New chintzes: all right, order new chintzes. Curtains and cushions and cosiness: all right, order them; have them mail my lawyer the bill.

You say you need a château: all right, have the château, my lawyers will fix it. Harvey kicked an armchair. It moved smoothly on its castors into place. Ruth, he thought, is fond of the baby. She adores Clara. Who wouldn't? But Clara belongs to me, that is, to my wife, Effie. No, Clara belongs to Ruth and depends on Ruth. It's good-bye, good-bye, to Clara. He looked at his watch. Time to telephone Toronto, it's about ten in the morning there. The story of playboy Harvey Gotham and his terrorist connections is certainly featured in the Canadian press, on the radio, the television.

Anne-Marie had come in, shiny black short hair, shiny black eyes, clear face. She had a small waist, stout hips. She carried a transistor radio playing rock music softly enough not to justify complaint.

"Do you know how to get a number on the telephone, long-distance to Toronto?" Harvey said.

"Of course," said the policewoman.

He thought, as he gave her the number, she doesn't look like a police official, she looks like a maid. Bedworthy and married. She's somebody's wife. Every woman I have to do with is somebody's wife. Ruth, Job's wife, and Effie who is still my wife, and who is shooting up the supermarkets. Twelve people hurt and millions of francs' theft and damage. If the police don't soon get the gang there will be deaths; housewives, policemen, children murdered. Am I responsible for my wife's debts? Her wounded, her dead?

Anne-Marie had left the transistor while she went to telephone; the music had been interrupted and the low murmur of an announcement drew Harvey's attention; he caught the phrases: Terrorist organization . . . Errors of justice . . . ; he turned the volume up. It was a bulletin from FLE issued to a Paris news agency, vindicating its latest activities. The gang was going to liberate Europe from its errors. "Errors of society, errors of the system." Most of all, liberation from the diabolical institution of the *gendarmerie* and the brutality of the *Brigade Criminelle*. It was much the same as every other terrorist announcement Harvey had ever read. "The multinationals and the forces of the reactionary imperialist powers . . ." It was like an alarm clock that ceases to wake the sleeper who, having heard it morning after morning, simply puts out a hand and switches it off without even opening his eyes.

The bulletin was followed by an announcement that fifty inspectors of the *Brigade Criminelle* were now investigating FLE's activities in the Vosges where the terrorists were still believed to be hiding out. End of announcement: on with the music.

"Your call to Toronto," said Anne-Marie.

Ruth was to go to Paris and leave next morning, with Clara, for Canada. A Volvo pulled up at the door. When he had finished his call, Harvey saw two suitcases already packed in the hall. Those people work fast. "Not so fast," Harvey said to Anne-Marie. "The child's father might not agree to her going to Canada. We must get his permission."

"We have his permission. Mr. Howe will call you tonight. He has agreed with Scotland Yard."

"The press will be here any minute," said Harvey. "They'll see Madame and the baby driving off."

"No, the police have the road cordoned off. Madame and the child will leave by a back door, anyway." She went out and gave instructions to the driver of the Volvo, who took off, round to the back of the house.

Anne-Marie lifted one of the suitcases and gestured to Harvey to take the other. He followed her, unfamiliar with all the passages of his château, through a maze of grey kitchens, dairies and washhouses as yet unrestored. By a door leading to a vast and sad old plantation which must have once been a kitchen garden, Ruth stood, huddled in her sheepskin coat, crying, cuddling the baby.

"Is it to be Toronto?" she said.

"Oh, yes, you'll be met. Do you have the money with you?" Harvey had given her charge of a quantity of cash long before the trouble started.

"I've taken most of it."

"You'll be all right once you're at my Uncle Joe's."

"Who did you say I was?" she said.

"My sister-in-law."

"And Clara?"

"Your niece. Ernie Howe has given his permission—"

"Oh, I know. I spoke to him myself," she said.

"Nobody tells me anything," Harvey said.

"Will I like your Uncle Joe?"

"I hope so. If not, you can go to my Auntie Pet."

"What is 'Pet' short for?" said Ruth.

"I really don't know." He could see she wanted to delay the parting. "Ring me to-night from Paris," he said. He kissed Ruth and he kissed Clara, and practically pushed them towards Anne-Marie who had already seen the suitcases into the car, and was waiting for Ruth, almost taking her under arrest. With a hand under Ruth's arm she led her along the little path towards the wider path where the car waited. They were off. Ruth and Clara in the front seat beside the driver. They were like an affluent married couple and child. Anne-Marie came back to the house, closed and locked the back door. Harvey said, "You lead the way back. I'll follow you. I don't know my way about this place." She laughed.

Twenty minutes later the press were let in. "Quiet!" said Anne-Marie. "We have a baby in the house. You mustn't wake her."

Harvey, freshly and acutely aware of Clara's innocent departure, was startled for an instant, then remembered quickly that Ruth and Clara were gone in secret.

"Madame is resting, too," announced Anne-Marie, "please, gentlemen, ladies, no noise."

There were eighteen men, five women; the rest were at the road-block outside the house arguing vainly with the police. This, Harvey learned from the reporters themselves, who crowded into the living room. There was a predominance of French, British and Americans among them. Harvey scrutinized them, as best he could trying to guess which one of them was a police agent. A wiry woman of about fifty with a red face, broken-veined, and thin grey hair fluffed out and falling all over her face as if to make the most of it, seemed to him a possible *flic*, if only for the reason that unlike the others she seemed to have no-one to talk to.

"Mr. Gotham, when did you last see—"

"I will answer no questions," Harvey said, "until you stop these flash-photographs." He sat back in his chair with folded arms. "Stop," he said, "just stop. I'll answer questions first, if they're reasonable. Then you can take some photos. But not all at once. Kindly keep your voices down; as you've heard, there's a baby sleeping upstairs and a lady who needs a lot of rest." One of the reporters, slouching by the door, a large fair middle-aged man, was already taking notes. What of? The man's face seemed familiar to Harvey but he couldn't place it.

The French journalists were the most vociferous. "Do you know where your wife is?"—"How long has she been a member—"—"Your wife Effie's terrorist activities, do you ascribe them to a reaction against her wealthy matrimonial experience, with all the luxury and boredom that capitalism produces?"—"What exactly are the creed and aims of your religious group, Mr. Gotham?"

Harvey said, "One at a time, please."

"With all your prospects and holdings, you still believe in God, is that right?"—"Are you asking us to believe that you have come to this château to study the Bible?" —"Isn't it so that you originally lived in that little lodge at the end of the drive?"

"Yes," said Harvey, "I went to work down there."

"Where does your wife get the money for her terrorist activities?"

"I don't know that my wife is engaged in terrorist activities."

"But the police have identified her. Look, Mr. Gotham, those people of the FLE get their money from someplace." This came from a fat young American who spoke like a machine-gun.

"Would you mind speaking French so that we all know where we are?" said Harvey. A Frenchman swiftly came to his American colleague's aid, and repeated the question in French.

"Apparently they bomb supermarkets and rob the cash. Haven't you read the papers?" Harvey said.

"If your wife came in here with a sub-machine-gun right now—?"

"That is a hypothetical question," Harvey said. The question was asked by a timid young Asiatic type with fine features and a sad pallor, who had evidently been let in to the conference on a quota system. He looked puzzled. "Your question is all theory," Harvey said, to help him. The young man nodded wisely and made some notes. What notes?—God knows.

"Didn't you hear a registration in the police station of your wife's voice on a loudspeaker warning the people to leave the supermarket before the bombing?—Surely you recognized your wife's voice?" said an American.

"I heard no registration. But if my wife should happen to give a warning to anyone in danger at any time, that would be very right of her, I think," Harvey said.

Most of the reporters were younger than Harvey. One, a bearded Swede, was old, paunchy. He alone seemed to know what the *Book of Job* was. He asked Harvey, "Would you say that you yourself are in the position of Job, in so far as you are a suspicious character in the eyes of the world, yet feel yourself to be perfectly innocent?"

Harvey saw his chance and took it: "I am hardly in the position of Job. He was covered with boils, for one thing, which I am not. And his friends, merely on the basis of his suffering, accused him of having sinned in some way. What Job underwent was tantamount to an interrogation by the Elders of his community. I intend no personal analogy. But I am delighted to get down at last to the subject of this conference: what was the answer to Job's question? Job's question was, why does God cause me to suffer when I've done nothing to deserve it? Now, Job was in no doubt whatsoever that his sufferings came from God and from no other source. The very rapidity with which one calamity followed upon another, shattering Job's world, leaving him destitute, bereft and sick all in a short space of time, gave dramatic evidence that the cause was not natural, but supernatural. The supernatural, with power to act so strongly and disastrously, could only, in Job's mind, be God. And we know he was right in the context of the book, because in the Prologue, you read specifically that it was God who brought up the subject of Job to Satan; it was God, in fact, who tempted Satan to torment Job, not Satan who tempted God. I'm afraid my French version of the scriptures isn't to hand, it's down in my study in the cottage, or I'd quote you the precise passage. But—"

"Mr. Gotham," said a young English woman dressed entirely in dark grey leather, "I'm sorry to interrupt but I have to file my story at six. Is it true that Nathan Fox is your wife's lover?"

"Please stick to French if you can. Anyway, I am addressing this gentleman," said Harvey, indicating the elderly Swede, "on a very important subject and—"

"Oh, no, Mr. Gotham. Oh, no." This was a tough pressman, indeterminately British or American, who spoke with a loud, fierce voice. "Oh, no, Mr. Gotham. You're here to answer our questions."

"Keep your voice down, please. The fact is that I am here because it is my home. You are here to listen to me. The subject is the *Book of Job* to which I have dedicated many years of my life. This gentleman," said Harvey, nodding to the grave and rather flattered Swede, "has asked me an interesting question on the subject. I have answered his question and I am elaborating on it. Your chance, and that of your colleagues, to put further questions will come in due course. As I was about to remark, Job's problem was partly a lack of knowledge. He was without access to any system of study which would point to the reason for his afflictions. He said specifically, 'I desire to reason with God,' and expected God to come out like a man and state his case."

"Mr. Gotham—"

"Mr. Gotham, can you state if you would side with your wife in any sense if she came up for trial? Do you yourself feel politically that the FLE have something to offer the young generation?"—This was from a lanky French journalist with bright eyes and a wide smile. He was rather a sympathetic type, Harvey thought, probably new to his trade.

"I'm really sorry to disappoint you," said Harvey with some charm, "but I'm giving you a seminar on *Job* without pay."

A hubbub had now started to break out. Protests and questions came battering in on Harvey from every side.

"Quiet!" bawled Harvey. "Either you listen to me in silence or you all go. Job's problem, as I was saying, was partly a lack of knowledge. Everybody talked but nobody told him anything about the reason for his sufferings. Not even God when he appeared. Our limitations of knowledge make us puzzle over the cause of suffering, maybe it is the cause of suffering itself. Quiet, over there! The baby's asleep. And I said, no photographs at present. As I say, we are plonked here in the world and nobody but our own kind can tell us anything. It isn't enough. As for the rest, God doesn't tell. No, I've already told you that I don't know where my wife is. How the *Book of Job* got into the holy scriptures I really do not know. That's the greatest mystery of all. For it doesn't—"

"Mr. Gotham," said the tough pressman, "the FLE

have held up supermarkets, jewellers and banks at Gérardmer, La Bresse, Rambervillers, Mirecourt and Baccarat. Your wife is—"

"You've left out Epinal," said Harvey. Cameras flashed. "Will you allow me to continue to answer the question put to me, or will you go?"

"Your wife—" . . . "Your background, Mr. Gotham —" . . . "Your wife's sister—"

"Conference over," said Harvey.

"Oh, no."—"No, Mr. Gotham."—"Wait a minute." Some were swearing and cursing; some were laughing.

But Harvey got up and made for the door. Most of the reporters were on their feet, very rowdy. The wiry red-faced woman, the possible police agent, sat holding her tape-recorder modestly on her lap. The large fair man at the door had grabbed a belt as if from nowhere and was fastening it rapidly round his waist. Harvey saw that it was packed neatly with cartridges and that a revolver hung from a holster, with the man's hand on it. He recognized him now as the sandy-haired policeman who, in uniform, had sat at the table throughout his interrogation at Epinal.

Harvey said, "I must tell you that there is a policeman in the room."

"What police? *La Brigade antigang?*"

"I have no idea what variety. Kindly leave quietly and in order, and don't wake the baby."

They left without order or quietness.

"Why don't you get out while you can? Get back to Canada," said a girl.—"We'll be seeing you in the court-room," said another. Some joked as they left, some over-turned chairs as they went. From everywhere came the last-minute flashes of the cameras recording the policeman, the overturned chairs, and recording Harvey standing in the middle of it, an image to be reproduced in one of next morning's papers under the title "Don't Wake the Baby." But at last they had gone. The wiry red-faced woman said sadly to Harvey as she passed him, "I'm afraid you'll get a very bad press."

The policeman followed them out and chivied them down the drive from his car. Before he shut the door Harvey noticed something new in the light cast from the hall: a washing-line had been slung well in evidence of the front portico. Anne-Marie had just finished taking baby clothes from it, had evidently been photographed doing so. She came towards him.

"Not very convincing," Harvey said. "Nobody hangs washing within sight of the approach to a château."

"Nobody used to," Anne-Marie said. "They do now. We, for example, are doing it. Nobody will find it in the least suspect."

"Didn't she tell you the hotel where she was going to in Paris?" Harvey said.

"Not me," said Anne-Marie. "I think she'll ring you if she said she would. In any case, the inspector is sure to know where she's staying."

It was nine-thirty, and Anne-Marie was leaving for the night, anxious about being extraordinarily late in returning home; she lived several miles away. A car driven by a plain-clothes policeman was waiting at the door. She hurried away, banged the car door, and was off.

Stewart Cowper had arrived about an hour before, full of travel-exasperation and police-harassment; he had been frisked and questioned at the entrance to the house; he had been travelling most of the day and he was cold. At present he was having a shower.

Harvey and Anne-Marie had together put the living room to rights. Ruth had not yet rung him from Paris as she had promised. Where was she? Harvey then noticed something new in the room, a large bowl of early spring flowers, professionally arranged, beautiful. Irises, jonquils, lilies, daffodils; all too advanced to be local products; they must have come from an expensive shop in Nancy. Anne-Marie must have put them there at some time between the clearing up of the mess and her leaving, but Harvey hadn't noticed them. They stood on a low round table, practically covering it as the outward leaves of the arrangement bent gracefully over the edge of the bowl. Harvey hadn't noticed them, either, while he was sitting having a drink with Stewart, trying to calm him down, nor while Anne-Marie, anxious about the time, laid out a cold supper that was still sitting on the small dining-table, waiting for Stewart to wash and change. Where did those flowers come from? Who brought them, who sent them? Anne-Marie hadn't left the house. And why should she order flowers?

Stewart came in and went to get himself another drink. He was a man of medium height, in his mid-forties with a school-boy's round face and round blue eyes; but this immature look was counteracted by a deep and expressive quality in his voice, so that as soon as he spoke the total effect was of a certain maturity and intelligence, cancelling that silly round-eyed look.

"Did you bring these flowers?" said Harvey.

"Did I bring what?"

"These flowers—I don't know where they've come

from. The maid—and by the way she's a policewoman —must have put them there some time this evening. But why?"

Stewart brought his drink to the sofa and sat sipping it.

Harvey's mind was working fast, and faster. "I think I know why they're there. Have you ever heard of a vase of flowers being bugged?"

"Rather an obvious way to plant a bug if the flowers weren't there already," said Stewart.

But Harvey was already pulling the flower-arrangement to bits. He shook each lily, each daffodil; he tore at the petals of the irises. Stewart drank his drink and told Harvey to calm down; he watched Harvey with his big blue eyes and then took another sip. Harvey splashed the water from the bowl all over the table and the floor. "I don't see anything," he said.

"From what I understand the police have had every opportunity to plant bugs elsewhere in the house; they need not introduce a bunch of flowers for the purpose," Stewart said. "What a mess you've made of a lovely bunch of flowers."

"I'd take you out to dinner," said Harvey. He sat on the sofa with his dejected head in his hands. He looked up. "I'd take you out to eat but I've got to wait in for a call from Ruth. She's in Paris but I don't know where. I've got to let my uncle in Toronto know the time of her arrival and her flight number. Did I tell you that she's taking the baby to my Uncle Joe's?"

"No," said Stewart.

"Well, she is. I've got to arrange for her to be met, and get through to Toronto and give them reasonable notice. And I've got to have a call from Ernie Howe, I think. At least he said he'd ring."

"How many other things have you got to do?"

"I don't know."

"Why don't you relax? You're in a hell of a state."

"I know. What are you supposed to be doing here?"

"Giving you some advice," Stewart said. "Of course, I can't act for you here in France."

"I don't need anyone. I've got what's-his-name in Paris if necessary."

"Martin Deschamps?—I've been in touch with him. He can't act for you in a case like this. No-one in his firm can, either. That means they won't. Terrorism is too unladylike for those fancy lawyers. I'm hungry."

"Let's sit down, then," said Harvey; they sat at the table to eat the cold supper. Harvey's hand shook as he started to pour the wine. He stopped and looked at his hand. "I'm shaking," he said. "I wonder why Ruth hasn't rung?"

Stewart took the bottle from him and poured out the wine. "Your nerves," he said.

"She must have had her dinner and put the baby to bed by now," Harvey said. "I'll give it another hour, then I'm going to ring the police and find out where she is. Ernie Howe should have rung, too."

"Maybe she didn't stop over in Paris. Perhaps she went straight to the airport."

"She should have rung. She could have been taken ill. She's pregnant."

"Is she?"

"So she says."

The telephone rang. An inspector of police. "M.

Gotham?—I want to let you know that Mme. Ruth Jansen has arrived in London."

"In London? I thought she was going to stop overnight in Paris. I've arranged for her to go to Canada to my—"

"She changed her mind."

"Where is she in London?"

"I can't tell you. Good night."

"If she didn't ring you as promised," said Stewart the next morning, "and Ernie Howe didn't ring you as promised, and if, in addition, it transpires she went to London, I should have thought you would suspect that the two were together."

"You think she has gone to Ernie Howe? Why should she go to him? She is pregnant by me."

"She has Ernie Howe's baby in her arms. It would be natural to take her to the father. You can't possess everything, Harvey."

"Do you know more than you say?" said Harvey.

"No, it's only a supposition."

"I'll ring Ernie Howe's flat as soon as my call to Canada has come through. It's hard on my uncle, mucking him about like this. He's not so young. I've just put through a call."

"It's the middle of the night in Toronto," said Stewart.

"I don't care."

Anne-Marie arrived in her thick coat, scarves and boots. "Good morning," she said, and then gave a pained wail. Her eyes were on the flowers that she had left in such a formal display the night before, now all pulled to pieces, even the petals torn to bits.

"I was looking for an electronic bug," Harvey said.

"I think you are not human," said Anne-Marie. She was now in tears, aimlessly lifting a daffodil, putting it down, then a blue, torn iris.

"Who ordered them, who sent them?" said Harvey.

Stewart said, "I'll help to clear the mess. Leave it to me."

"I had them sent myself," said Anne-Marie. "To give you some joy after your ordeal with the press and your loss of the baby. My sister-in-law has a flower shop and I made a special-messenger arrangement with her for the most beautiful flowers; a personal present. I thought that with the loss of Madame and Clara you would enjoy those lovely spring flowers."

Stewart had his arm round the police agent's shoulders. "His nerves gave way," said Stewart. "That's all."

The telephone rang; Harvey's call to Canada. It was a sleepy manservant who answered, as Harvey had counted on. He was able to explain, without having to actually talk to his uncle, that Ruth and the baby were probably not coming after all, and that any references to him in the newspapers and on the television were probably false.

He put down the receiver. The telephone rang: "Hallo, Harvey!" The telephone rang off. Again it rang: "Harvey, it's Ruth." She was speaking in a funny way. She was calling herself Ree-uth, although definitely the voice was hers. It must be the London influence, Harvey registered all in a moment. But she was going on. "I changed my mind, Harvey. I had to bring Clara [pronounced Clah-rah] to her father [pronounced fah-thah]."

"What are you saying?" said Harvey. "You mean you're not going to my Uncle Joe in Toronto. You've decided to shack down with Ernie Howe, is that it?"

"That's it," said Ruth.

"Then I think you might have had enough considera-
tion for my Uncle Joe—he's seventy-eight—to let me
know."

"Oh, I was busy with Clah-rah."

"Pass me Ernie," said Harvey.

"Ernie, do you mind?" said Ruth's voice, apart.

"Hallo," said the other voice.

"Ernie Howe?"

"That's me."

"What are you doing with Ruth?"

"We've just had a tunah-fish salad. We fed Clah-rah."

Harvey then remembered Ernie's voice; (that's where
Ruth got the Clah-rah).

"I make a good fah-thah," said Ernie; "and I don't like
your tone of superiority."

After a great many more hot words, Harvey began to
recollect, at the back of his mind, that he really had no
rights in the matter; not much to complain of at all. He
said good night, hung up, and returned to the sitting
room hoping for some consolation from his friend.

His friend was sitting on the sofa holding hands with
Anne-Marie. Harvey was in time to hear him say, "May
I fall in love with you?"

"She's married," said Harvey in English.

"Not at all," said Anne-Marie in her most matter-of-
fact voice. "I live with my married brother."

"Well, I thought you were married," said Harvey.

"That's when you thought I was a maid."

"If you're not a maid then what are you doing here?"
said Harvey.

"He's exasperated," said Stewart. "Don't mind him."

Anne-Marie took a long glance at the disorderly table

of ruined flowers and said, "I have to remain here on duty. I'm going to make the coffee."

When she had left, Harvey said, "You're behaving like an undergraduate who's just put foot on the Continent for the first time, meeting his first Frenchwoman."

"What was the news from England?"

"Ruth is with Ernie Howe."

"What do the newspapers say?"

"I don't know. Find out; it's your job."

"Is it?" said Stewart.

"If it isn't, what are you doing here?"

"I suppose I'm just a comforter," Stewart said.

"I suppose you are."

VIII

"Is it possible," said Harvey, "for anyone to do something perfectly innocent but altogether unusual, without giving rise to suspicion?"

Stewart said, "Not if his wife is a terrorist."

"Assume that she is not."

"All right, I assume. But here you were in a small hamlet in France, a rich man living in primitive conditions. Well, nobody bothered you until the police began to suspect a link between you and the FLE a certain time ago, and even then they only had you under surveillance, from a distance; they didn't haul you in immediately or harass you so that your life was uncomfortable. You weren't even aware of their presence till lately. And now you've been questioned, grilled; it's only natural. It might have been worse. Much worse. You don't know the police."

"My papers have been scrutinized, all my work, my private things—"

"I can't sympathize too much, Harvey. I can't say you've really suffered. These police obviously are going carefully with you. They're protecting you from the mob, the phone calls. They probably believe you; they know by now, I should think, that you have no contact with Effie. I think they're right to watch out in case she has any contact with you."

"You are wrong," said Harvey, "to say that I haven't suffered. Did you hear the press round-up on the radio this morning?—My name's worse than Effie's in the eyes of the press."

The local newspaper, the only one so far to arrive in his hands, was on the coffee-table in front of them, with the front page uppermost. The headline, "The Guru of the Vosges," stretched above a picture of Harvey, distraught, in his sitting room of final disorder at the press conference. Under the picture was the title-paragraph of the subsequent article:

> Harvey Gotham, the American "prophet," inveighing against God, who he claims has unjustly condemned the world to suffering. *God is a Shit* was one of the blasphemies preached at an international press conference held yesterday in his 40-roomed château recently acquired by this multi-millionaire husband of the gangster-terrorist Effie Gotham, leading activist of FLE.

In the article, the writer of it reflected on the influence of Harvey on a girl like Effie "from the poorer classes of

London," and on her sister and an infant, Clara, still under his control at the château.

Harvey said to Stewart, "I never once said *'Dieu est merde.'* "

"Maybe you implied it."

"Perhaps I did. But I did not speak as a prophet; I discussed some aspects of *Job* in an academic sense."

"For a man of your intelligence, you are remarkably stupid," said Stewart. "It's Effie they wanted news of. Failing that, they made the best of what they got. You should have let Effie divorce you with a huge settlement a long time ago. She can get a divorce any time; it's the money she wanted."

"To finance FLE?"

"You asked me to assume she isn't involved."

"I don't want to divorce Effie. I don't want a divorce."

"Are you still in love with Effie?"

"Yes."

"Then you're an unhappy man. Why did you leave her?"

"I couldn't stand her sociological clap-trap. If she wanted to do some good in the world she had plenty of opportunity. There was nothing to stop her taking up charities and causes; she could have had money for them, and she always had plenty of time. But she has to rob supermarkets and banks and sleep with people like *that*." He pointed to a row of photographs in the paper. Three young men and Effie. The photograph of Effie was that which the police had found among his papers. Harvey told Stewart this, and said, "They don't seem to have any other picture of Effie. I wonder how they got photos of her friends."

"In the same way that they got Effie's, I expect.

Through rummaging in the homes of their families, their girl-friends."

"What can she see in them?" Harvey said. Stewart turned the paper round to see it better. One of the men was dressed in a very padded-shouldered coat, a spotted bow tie and hair falling down past the point where the picture ended, which was just above his elbow; the second man was a blond, blank-faced boy with thick lips; the third seemed to be positively posing as the criminal he was alleged to be, being sneery, narrow-eyed and double-chinned, and bearing a two-day stubble beard. There was Effie amongst them, looking like Effie. The men were identified by French names, Effie by the name of Effie Gotham, wife of the millionaire guru.

"What does she see in them?" demanded Harvey. "It's not so much that I'm jealous as that I'm intellectually insulted by the whole thing. I always have been by Effie's attitude to life. I thought she'd grow out of it."

"I am to assume that Effie is not involved," said Stewart.

"Well, there's her picture along with the others. It's difficult for me to keep up the fiction," Harvey said.

"Do you mean that the photograph convinces you?" Stewart said. "You know where the police got the photograph. Out of a drawer in your desk."

"It wasn't exactly out of a drawer in a desk," Harvey said. "It was out of a box. I keep things in boxes down there in my working cottage. I'll take you to see it. I haven't been back to the cottage since I was arrested in Epinal three days ago."

"Were you really arrested?"

"Perhaps not technically. I was definitely invited to come along to the commissariat. I went."

"I wonder," said Stewart, "why there's been so little in the press about Nathan Fox. I only heard on the radio that he'd disappeared suddenly from your house. And they don't include him in the gang. Maybe they couldn't find a photograph of him. A photo makes a gangster real."

"There was an identikit of Effie in the papers the day I was hauled in," said Harvey.

"Did it look like Effie?"

"I'm afraid so. In fact it looked like Ruth. But it would pass for Effie. It looked like Job's wife, too. You know, it was a most remarkable thing, Stewart, I was sitting in the museum at Epinal reflecting on that extraordinary painting of Job and his wife by Georges de La Tour, when suddenly the police—"

"You told me that last night," said Stewart.

"I know. I want to talk about it."

"Don't you think," said Stewart, "that it would be odd if Effie wanted alimony from you simply to finance the FLE, when she could have sold her jewellery?"

"Hasn't she done that?"

"No, it's still in the safety-box at the bank. I hold the second key. There's still enough money in her bank to meet the standing orders for insurances and charities. Nothing's changed."

"Well, why did she want to fleece me?"

"I don't see why she shouldn't have tried to get maintenance of some sort from you. It's true that her child by Ernie Howe damaged her case. But you walked out on her. She behaved like a normal woman married to a man in your position."

"Effie is not a normal woman," said Harvey.

"Oh, if you're talking in a basic sense, what woman is?"

"Women who don't get arrested in Trieste for shop-lifting are normal," said Harvey. "Especially women with her kind of jewellery in the bank. Whose side are you on, anyway, mine or Effie's?"

"In a divorce case, that is the usual question that the client puts, sooner or later. It's inevitable," said the lawyer.

"But this is something different from a divorce case. Don't you realize what's happened?"

"I'm afraid I do," said Stewart.

Next day was a Saturday. They sat in Harvey's cottage, huddling over the stove because the windows had been opened to air the place. There had been a feeling of spring in the early March morning, but this had gone by eleven o'clock; it was now winter again, bleak, with a slanting rain. As Harvey unlocked the door of his little house Stewart said, "Lousy soil you've got here. Nothing much growing."

"I haven't bothered to cultivate it."

"It's better up at the château."

"Oh, yes, it's had more attention."

This was Harvey's first visit to the cottage since the police had pounced. He looked round carefully, opening the windows upstairs and downstairs, while Stewart lit the stove. "They haven't changed the décor," Harvey said. "But a few bundles of papers are not in the places I left them in. Shifted, a matter of inches—but I know, I know."

"Have they taken any of your papers, letters, business documents?"

"What letters and business papers? You have the letters and the business papers. All I have are my notes, and the manuscript of my little book, so far as it goes— it's to be a monograph, you know. I don't know if they've subtracted the few files, but they could have photographed them; much good might it do them. Files of notes on the *Book of Job*. They did take the photograph of Effie; that, they did take. I want it back."

"You're entitled to ask for it," said Stewart.

From the window, a grey family Citroën could be seen parked round a bend in the path, out of sight of the road; in it were two men in civilian clothes occupying the front seats. The rain plopped lazily on to the roof of the car and splashed the windscreen. "Poor bastards," Harvey said. "They do it in three- or four-hour shifts."

"Well, it's a protection for you, anyway. From the press if not from the terrorists."

"I wish I was without the need for protection, and I wish you were in your office in London."

"I don't go to the office on Saturday," Stewart said.

"What do you do at the week-ends?"

"Fuck," said Stewart.

"Do you mean, fuck the question or that on Saturdays and Sundays you fuck?"

"Both."

"Don't you ever go to a concert or a film on Sundays? Never go to Church?"

"Sometimes I go to a concert. I go away for the week-ends, often. I do the usual things."

"Well, you're wasting your time here," Harvey said.

"No, because first you're my most valuable client.

That's from a practical point of view. And secondly, I'm interested in your *Book of Job*; it just beats me how a man of your scope should choose to hide himself away in this hole. And thirdly, of course, I'm a friend; I want to see you out of this mess. I strongly advise you to come back to London here and now. Do you have your passport?"

"Yes, they gave me back my passport."

"Oh, they took it away?"

"Yes, they took the stuff out of my pockets," Harvey said. "They gave it all back. I'm not leaving."

"Why?"

"Well, all my books and things are here. I don't see why I should run away. I intend to go on as usual. Besides, I'm anxious about Effie."

"Maybe Effie would move to another field of action if you weren't in the Vosges," said Stewart. "You see, I don't want you to become an unwilling accomplice."

"Effie follows the gang," said Harvey.

"Doesn't she lead it?"

"Oh, I don't know. I don't even know for certain that she's in it. It's all mere allegation on the part of the police."

Stewart walked about the little room, with his scarf wound round his neck. "It's chilly," he said. He was looking at the books. "Does Anne-Marie cook for you?" he said.

"Yes, indifferently. She's a police agent by profession."

"Oh that doesn't mean much," said Stewart, "when you know that she is."

"I used to love mealtimes with Effie," said Harvey. "I enjoyed the mealtimes more than the meals."

"Let's go out somewhere for lunch," said Stewart.

"We can go in to Nancy. Undoubtedly we'd be followed."

"That doesn't mean much if you know you are being followed," said Stewart.

Harvey stood in the middle of the room watching with an irritated air while Stewart fingered his books.

"There's nothing of interest," said Harvey, "unless you're interested in the subject."

"Well, you know I am. I still don't see why you can't write your essay elsewhere."

"I've got used to it here."

"Would you like to have Ruth back?" said Stewart.

"Not particularly. I would like to have Clara back."

"With Effie?"

"No, Effie isn't a motherly type."

"Ruth is a mother?"

"She is a born children's nurse."

"But you would like to have Effie back?" Stewart said, and he made light of this, as of all his questions, by putting them simultaneously with a flicking-through of the pages of Harvey's books.

"Yes, I would; in theory," said Harvey. "That is the *New English Bible*. The translation is godforsaken."

"Then you'd be willing to take Ruth back if she brought Clara. But you'd prefer to have Effie to make love to?"

"That is the unattainable ideal. The *New English Bible*'s version of *Job* makes no distinction between Behemoth and Leviathan. They translate the two as 'the crocodile,' which has of course some possibility as a theory, but it simply doesn't hold in the context."

"I thought Behemoth was the hippopotamus," said Stewart.

"Well, that's the general view, not necessarily correct. However, the author of *Job* turns God into a poet at that point, proclaiming wonderful hymns to his own creation, the buffalo, the ostrich, the wild ass, the horse, the eagle; then there's the sparrow-hawk. And God says consider this, look at that, reflect on their ways, how they live and survive; I did it all; where were you when I did it? Finally come Behemoth and Leviathan. Well, if you are going to translate both Behemoth and Leviathan as the crocodile, it makes far too long a passage, it gives far more weight to the crocodile as one of God's marvels than is obviously intended. As for the features of Behemoth, they fit in with the hippopotamus or some large and similar creature equally as well as with the crocodile. Why should God be so proud of his crocodile that he devotes thirty-eight verses to it, and to the horse only seven?"

"There must be some good arguments in favour of Behemoth and Leviathan both being the crocodile, though," Stewart said.

"Of course there are arguments. The scholars try to rationalize *Job* by rearranging the verses where there is obviously no sense in them. Sometimes, of course, the textual evidence irresistibly calls for a passage to be moved from the traditional place to another. But moving passages about for no other reason than that they are more logical is no good for the *Book of Job*. It doesn't make it come clear. The *Book of Job* will never come clear. It doesn't matter; it's a poem. As for Leviathan and Behemoth, Lévêque, who is the best modern scholar on *Job,* distinguishes between the two." Harvey was apparently back in his element. He seemed to have forgotten about the police outside his house, and that Effie was a criminal at large.

Stewart said, "You amaze me."

"Why?"

"Don't you want to know the facts about Effie?"

"Oh, Effie."

Harvey had in his hands one of Lévêque's volumes. "He accepts Leviathan as the crocodile and Behemoth as the hippopotamus. He takes Behemoth to be a hippopotamus or at least a large beast."

"What about these other new Bibles?" said Stewart, pointing to a couple of new translations. He wondered if perhaps Harvey was not so guileless as he seemed. Stewart thought perhaps Harvey might really be involved with Effie and her liberation movement. There was something not very convincing about Harvey's cool-headedness.

"Messy," said Harvey. "They all try to reach everybody and end by saying nothing to anybody. There are no good new Bibles. The 1945 *Knox* wasn't bad but still obscure—it's a Vulgate translation, of course; the *Jerusalem Bible* and this *Good News Bible* are not much improvement on the old *Moffat.*"

"You stick to the *Authorized* then?"

"For my purpose, it's the best English basis. One can get to know the obvious mistakes and annotate accordingly."

Harvey poured drinks and handed one to Stewart.

"I think I can see," said Stewart, "that you're happy here. I didn't realize how much this work meant to you. It has puzzled me slightly; I knew you were dedicated to the subject but didn't understand how much, until I came here. You shouldn't think of marriage."

"I don't. I think of Effie."

"Only when you're not thinking of *Job?*"

"Yes. What can I do for her by thinking?"

"Your work here would make a good cover if you were in with Effie," said the lawyer.

"A very bad cover. The police aren't really convinced by my story. Why should you be?"

"Oh, Harvey, I didn't mean—"

Anne-Marie arrived with a grind of brakes in the little Renault. She left the car with a bang of the door and began to proclaim an urgency before she had opened the cottage gate.

"Mr. Gotham, a phone call from Canada."

Harvey went to open the door to her. "What is it from Canada?" he said.

"Your aunt on the telephone. She'll ring you back in ten minutes."

"I'll come up to the house right away."

To Stewart, he said, "Wait for me. I'll be back shortly and we'll go out to lunch. You know, there could have been an influence of *Prometheus* on *Job;* the dates could quite possibly coincide. But I find vast differences. Prometheus wasn't innocent, for one thing. He stole fire from Heaven. Job was innocent."

"Out to lunch!" said Anne-Marie. "I'm preparing lunch at the château."

"We'll have it cold for dinner," thundered Harvey as he got into the car. Anne-Marie followed him; looking back at Stewart who gave her a long smile full of what looked like meaning, but decidedly so unspecific as to mean nothing.

As they whizzed up the drive to the château Anne-Marie said, "You think because you are rich you can do anything with people. I planned a lunch."

"You should first have enquired whether we would be in for lunch," said Harvey.

"Oh, no," she said, with some point. "It was for you to say you would be out."

"I apologize."

"The apologies of the rich. They are cheap."

Half an hour went by before the telephone rang again. The police were vetting the calls, turning away half the world's reporters and others who wanted to speak to the terrorist's guru husband. Harvey therefore made no complaint. He sat in patience reading all about himself once more in the local morning newspaper until the telephone rang.

"Oh, it's you, Auntie Pet. It must be the middle of the night with you; how are you?"

"How are *you?*"

"All right."

"I saw you on the television and it's all in the paper. How could you blaspheme in that terrible way, saying those things about your Creator?"

"Auntie Pet, you've got to understand that I said nothing whatsoever about God, I mean our Creator. What I was talking about was a fictional character in the *Book of Job*, called God. I don't know what you've seen or read, but it's not yet proved finally that Effie, my wife, is a terrorist."

"Oh, Effie isn't involved, it goes without saying. I never said Effie was a terrorist, I know she isn't, in fact. What I'm calling about is this far more serious thing, it's a disgrace to the family. I mean, this is to blaspheme when you say that God is what you said He was."

"I never said what they said I said he was," said Harvey. "How are you, Auntie Pet? How is Uncle Joe?"

"Uncle Joe, I never hear from. But I get to know."

"And yourself? I haven't heard from you for ages."

"Well, I don't write much. The prohibitive price of stamps. My health is everything that can be expected by a woman who does right and fears the Lord. Your Uncle Joe just lives on there with old Collier who is very much to blame, too. Neither of them has darkened the door of the church for as long as I can remember. They are unbelievers like you."

"On the contrary, I have abounding faith."

"You shouldn't question the Bible. Job was a good man. There is a Christian message in the *Book of Job*."

"But Job didn't know that."

"How do you know? We have a lovely Bible, there. Why do you want to change it? You should look after your wife and have a family, and be a good husband, with all your advantages, and the business doing so well. Your Uncle Joe refused the merger."

"Well, Auntie Pet, it's been a pleasure to talk to you. I have to go out with my lawyer for lunch, now. I'm glad you managed to get my number so you could put your mind at rest."

"I got your number with the utmost difficulty."

"Yes, I was wondering how you got it, Auntie Pet."

"Money," said Auntie Pet.

"Ah," said Harvey.

"I'll be in touch again."

"Keep well. Don't take the slightest notice of what the newspapers and the television say."

"What about the radio?"

"Also, the radio."

"Are you starting a new religion, Harvey?"

"No."

Stewart and Harvey crossed the Place Stanislas at Nancy. The rain had stopped and a silvery light touched the gilded gates at the corners of the square, it glittered on the lamp-posts with their golden garlands and crown-topped heads, and on the bright and lacy iron-work of all the balconies of the *hôtel de ville*.

"The square always looks lovely out of season," said Stewart.

"It's supposed to have crowds," Harvey said. "That's what it was evidently made for."

Two police cars turned into the square and followed them at a crawl.

"The bistro I had in mind is down a narrow street," said Harvey. "Let them follow us there. The police have to eat, too."

But they had a snack-lunch in the police station at Nancy, two policemen having got out of their car and invited Harvey and Stewart to join them.

"What's the matter, now?" Harvey had said when the police approached them.

Stewart said, "I require an explanation."

The explanation was not forthcoming until they were taken later in the afternoon to the police headquarters in Epinal.

"A policeman has been killed in Paris."

IX

Stewart cowper, having invoked the British Consul, was allowed to leave the police headquarters the same afternoon that he was detained with Harvey. He refused to answer any questions at all, and his parting advice to Harvey was to do likewise. They were alone in a corridor.

"The least I can do," said Harvey, "is to defend Effie."

"Understandable," said Stewart, and left to collect his luggage from the château and get a hired car to Paris, and a plane to London.

Harvey got home later that night, having failed to elicit, from the questions he was asked by an officer who had come to Epinal for the purpose—the same old questions—what had exactly happened in Paris that morning, and where Effie was supposed to fit into the murder of the policeman.

"Did you hear about the killing on the radio, M. Gotham?"

"No. I've only just learned of it from you. I wasn't in the château this morning. I was in the cottage with my English lawyer, Stewart Cowper."

"What did you discuss with your lawyer?"

"The different versions of the *Book of Job* in various recent English translations of the Bible."

Harvey's interrogator looked at him with real rage. "One of our policemen has been killed," he said.

"I'm sorry to hear it," said Harvey.

They escorted him to pick up his car at Nancy, and followed him home.

Next day the Sunday papers had the same photograph of Effie. There was also a photograph of the policeman, lying in the street beside a police car, covered by a sheet, with some police standing by. Effie had been recognized by eye-witnesses at the scene of the killing, in the eighteenth *arrondissement*. A blonde, long-haired girl with a gun. She was the killer. Her hair was drawn back in a pony-tail at the time of the commando-raid; she was wearing blue jeans and a grey pullover. The Paris security police and the *gendarmerie* were now operating jointly in the search for FLE and its supporters, and especially for the Montmartre killers.

That was the whole of the news, though it filled several pages of the newspapers. The volume of printed words was to be explained by the length of the many paragraphs ending with a question mark, by numerous interpolations about Harvey and his Bible-sect, his wealth, his château, and by details of the unfortunate policeman's family life.

It was not till after lunch on Monday that he was invited to the commissariat at Epinal once more. Two security men from Paris had arrived to interrogate him. Two tall men, one of them in his late forties, robust, with silvering sideburns, the other fair and skinny, not much over thirty, with gilt-rimmed glasses, an intellectual. Harvey thought, if he had seen them together in a restaurant, he would have taken the older man for a businessman, the younger for a priest.

Later, when he chewed over their questions, he was to find it difficult to distinguish between this second interrogation and the first one of a few days ago. This was partly because the older man, who introduced himself by the name of Chatelain, spent a lot of time going over Harvey's previous deposition.

"My house is surrounded by your men," said Harvey. "You have your young woman auxiliary in my house. What are you accusing me of?" (Stewart Cowper had advised him: If they question you again, ask them what they have against you, demand to know what is the charge.)

"We are not accusing, Mr. Gotham, we are questioning."

"Questions can sound like accusations."

"A policeman has been shot dead."

And Harvey recalled later their continual probe into why he had settled in France:

"I liked the house," said Harvey, "I got my permit to stay in France. I'm regular with the police."

"Your wife has been in trouble before."

"I know," said Harvey.

"Do you love your wife?"

"That's rather a personal question."

"It was a personal question for the policeman who was killed."

"I wonder," said Harvey, conversationally. He was suddenly indignant and determined to be himself, thoughtfully in charge of his reasoning mind, not any sort of victim. "I wonder . . . I'm not sure that death is personal in the sense of being in love. So far as we know, we don't feel death. We know the fear of death, we know the process of dying. From the outside it looks the most personal of phenomena. But isn't death the very negation of the personal—therefore, strictly speaking, impersonal? A dead body is the most impersonal thing I can think of. Unless one believes in the continuity of personality in its terrestrially recognizable form, as opposed to life-after-death which is something else. Many disbelieve in life after death, of course, but—"

"*Pardon?* Are you trying to tell me that the death of one of our men is trivial?"

"No. I was reflecting on a remark of yours. Philosophizing, I'm afraid. I meant—"

"Kindly don't philosophize," said Chatelain. "This is not the place. I want to know where your wife is. Where is Effie?"

"I don't know where Mme. Gotham is."

And again:

"A policeman has been killed by the FLE gang. Two men and a girl, all armed. In the eighteenth *arrondissement* in Paris."

"I'm sorry that a policeman has been shot," said Harvey. "Why in the eighteenth *arrondissement?*"

"That's what we're asking you," said Chatelain.

"I have no idea. I thought these terrorists acted mainly in popular suburbs."

"Was your wife ever before in the eighteenth *arrondissement*, do you know?"

"Of course," said Harvey. "Who hasn't been in the eighteenth? It's Montmartre."

"Have you and your wife any friends there?"

"I have friends there and I suppose my wife has, too."

"Who are your friends?"

"You should know. Your colleagues here went through my address book last week and checked all my friends."

In the middle of the afternoon Chatelain became more confidential. He began to melt, but only in resemblance to a refrigerator which thaws when the current is turned off. True warmth, thought Harvey at the time, doesn't drip, drip, drip. And later, in his cottage, when he re-constituted the scene he thought: And I ask myself, why was he a refrigerator in the first place?

"Don't think I don't sympathize with you, Mr. Gotham," said Chatelain, on the defreeze. "Not to know where one's wife is cannot be a pleasant experience."

"Don't think I don't sympathize with you," said Harvey. "I know you've lost one of your men. That's serious. And I sympathize, as everyone should, with his family. But you offer no proof that my wife, Effie, is involved. You offer only a photograph that you confiscated from a box on my table."

"We confiscated . . . ?" The man consulted Harvey's thick file which lay on the desk. "Ah, yes. You are right. The Vosges police obtained that photograph from your house. Witnesses have identified the girl in the gang from the photograph. And look—the identikit, constructed with the help of eye-witnesses to a bank robbery and supermarket bombings, some days prior to our obtaining the photograph. Look at it—isn't that your wife?"

Harvey looked at the drawing.

"When I first saw it in the paper I thought it resembled my wife's sister, Ruth, rather than my wife," he said. "Since it couldn't possibly refer to Ruth it seems to me even more unlikely that it refers to Effie."

"Mme. Gotham was arrested in Trieste."

Harvey was still looking at the identikit. It reminded him, now, of Job's wife in La Tour's painting even though the drawing was full-face and the painting showed a profile.

"She was arrested for shoplifting," said Harvey.

"Why did she do that?"

Harvey put down the identikit and gave Chatelain his attention. "I don't know that she did it. If she did, it does not follow that she bombs supermarkets and kills policemen."

"If I was in your place," said Chatelain, "I would probably speak as you do. But if you were in my place, you would press for some indication, any indication, any guess, as to where she is. I don't blame you for trying to protect your wife. You see," he said, leaning back in his chair and looking away from Harvey, towards the window, "a policeman has been shot dead. His wife is in a shop on the outskirts of Paris where they live, a popular quarter, with her twelve-year-old daughter who has a transistor radio. The lady is waiting her turn at the cash-desk. The child draws her mother's attention to a flash item of news that has interrupted the music. A policeman has been shot and killed in the eighteenth *arron-*

dissement; the name is being withheld until the family can be informed. The assassins, two men and a girl, have escaped. The terrorist gang FLE have immediately telephoned the press to claim the crime. The main points of the news flash are repeated: A policeman killed, leaving a wife and two daughters aged fourteen and twelve. Now this lady, the policeman's wife, is always worried when she hears of the death or wounding of a policeman. In this case the description is alarmingly close. The eighteenth *arrondissement* where her husband is on duty; the ages of their daughters. She hurries home and finds a police car outside her block of flats. It is indeed her husband who has been killed. Did she deserve this?"

"No," said Harvey. "Neither did the policeman. We do not get what we merit. The one thing has nothing to do with the other. Your only course is to prevent it happening again."

"Depend on us," said the policeman.

"If I may say so," said Harvey, "you are wasting efforts on me which might profitably be directed to that end."

"Any clue, any suggestion . . ." said Chatelain, with great patience. He almost pleaded. "Are there any houses in Paris that you know of, where they might be found?"

"None," said Harvey.

"No friends?"

"The few people I know with establishments in Paris are occupied with business affairs in rather a large, multinational way. I don't believe they would like the FLE."

"Nathan Fox is a good housekeeper?"

"I believe he can be useful in a domestic way."

"He could be keeping a safe house for the gang in Paris."

139

"I don't see him as the gangster type. Honestly, you know, I don't think he's in it."

"But your wife . . . She is different?"

"I didn't say so."

"And yourself?"

"What about myself? What are you asking?" Harvey said.

"You have a connection with the gang?"

"No."

"Why did you hang baby clothes on the line outside your cottage as early as last spring?" said Chatelain next.

Harvey was given a break at about seven in the evening. He was accompanied to a café for a meal by the tall young Parisian inspector with metal-rimmed glasses, Louis Pomfret by name.

Pomfret spoke what could be described as "perfect English," that awful type of perfect English that comes over Radio Moscow. He said something apologetic, in semi-disparagement of the police. Harvey couldn't now remember the exact words. But he recalled Pomfret remarking, too, on the way to the café, "You must understand that one of their men has been killed." ("Their" men, not "our" men, Harvey noted.)

At the café table the policeman told Harvey, "A Canadian lady arrived in Paris who attempted to reach you on the telephone, and we intercepted her. She's your aunt. We've escorted her safely to the château where she desired to go."

"God, it's my Aunt Pet. Don't give her any trouble."

"But, no."

If you think you'll make me grateful for all this courtesy, thought Harvey, you are mistaken. He said, "I should hope not."

The policeman said, "I'm afraid the food here is ghastly."

"They make a good omelette. I've eaten here before," said Harvey.

Ham omelettes and wine from the Vosges.

"It's unfortunate for you, Gotham," said Pomfret, "but you appreciate, I hope, our position."

"You want to capture these members of the FLE before they do more damage."

"Yes, we do. And of course, we will. Now that a member of the police has been killed . . . You appreciate, his wife was shopping in a supermarket with her son of twelve, who had a transistor radio. She was taking no interest in the programme. At one point the boy said—"

"Are you sure it was a boy?" Harvey said.

"It was a girl. How do you know?"

"The scene has been described to me by your colleague."

"You're very observant." Pomfret smiled, quite nicely.

"Well, of course I'm observant in a case like this," said Harvey. "I'm hanging on your lips."

"Why?"

"To hear if you have any evidence that my wife is involved with a terrorist gang."

"We have a warrant for her arrest," said Pomfret.

"That's not evidence."

"I know. But we don't put out warrants without reason. Your wife was arrested in Trieste. She was definitely lodging there with a group which has since been identified as members of the FLE gang. When the police photograph from the incident at Trieste noticeably resembled the photograph we obtained from you, and also resembled the identikit made up from eye-witnesses of the bombings and incursions here in France, we call that sufficient evidence to regard your wife as a suspect."

"I would like to see the photograph from Trieste," said Harvey. "Why haven't I been shown it?"

"You are not investigating the case. We are."

"But I'm interested in her whereabouts," Harvey said. "What does this photograph from the police at Trieste look like?"

"It's an ordinary routine photograph that's taken of all people under arrest. Plain and flat, like a passport photograph. It looks like your wife. It's of no account to you."

"Why wasn't I shown it, told about it?"

"I think you can see it if you want."

"Your people at the commissariat evidently don't believe me when I say I don't know where Effie is."

"Well, I suppose that's why you've been questioned. You've never been officially convoked."

"The English word is summoned."

"Summoned; I apologize."

"Lousy wine," said Harvey.

"It's what you get in a cheap café," said Pomfret.

"They had better when I ate here before," said Harvey. "Look, all you've got to go on is an identikit made in France which resembles two photographs of my wife."

"And the address she was residing at in Trieste. That's most important of all."

"She is inclined to take up with unconventional people," said Harvey.

"Evidently, since she married yourself."

"Do you know," said Harvey, "I'm very conventional, believe it or not."

"I don't believe it, of course."

"Why?"

"Your mode of life in France. For an affluent man to establish himself in a cottage and study the *Book of Job* is not conventional."

"Job was an affluent man. He sat among the ashes. Some say, on a dung-heap outside the city. He was very conventional. So much so that God was bored with him."

"Is that in the scriptures?" said the policeman.

"No, it's in my mind."

"You've actually written it down. They took photo-copies of some of your pages."

"I object to that. They had no right."

"It's possible they had no right. Why have you never brought in a lawyer?"

"What for?"

"Exactly. But it would be the conventional thing to do."

"I hope you're impressed," said Harvey. "You see, if I were writing a film-script or a pornographic novel, you wouldn't find it so strange that I came to an out-of-the-way place to work. It's the subject of *Job* you can't understand my giving my time to."

"More or less. I think, perhaps, you've been trying to put yourself in the conditions of Job. Is that right?"

"One can't write an essay on *Job* sitting round a swimming pool in a ten-acre park, with all that goes with it. But I could just as well study the subject in a quiet apartment in some city. I came to these parts because I happened to find the cottage. There is a painting of Job and his wife here in Epinal which attracts me. You should see it."

"I should," said Pomfret. "I shall."

"Job's wife looks remarkably like my wife. It was painted about the middle of the seventeenth century so it can't be Effie, if that's what you're thinking."

"We were discussing Job, not Mme. Effie."

"Then what am I doing here," said Harvey, "being interrogated by you?"

Pomfret remained good-natured. He said something about their having a supper and a talk, not an interrogation. "I am genuinely interested," said Pomfret, "speaking for myself. You are isolated like Job. But you haven't lost your goods and fortune. Any possibility of that?"

"No, but I'm as good as without them here. More so before I took the château."

"Oh, I was forgetting the château. I've only seen your cottage, from the outside. It looks impoverished enough."

"It was the boils that worried Job."

"*Pardon?* The boils?"

"Boils. Skin-sores. He was covered with them."

"Ah, yes, that is correct. Don't you, like Job, feel the need of friends to talk to in your present troubles?"

"One thing that the *Book of Job* teaches us," Harvey said, "is the futility of friendship in times of trouble. That is perhaps not a reflection on friends but on friendship. Friends mean well, or make as if they do. But friendship itself is made for happiness, not trouble."

"Is your aunt a friend?"

"My Aunt Pet, who you tell me has arrived at the château?—I suppose she thinks of herself as a friend.

She's a bore, coming at this moment. At any moment.
—You don't suppose this is anything but an interrogation, do you? Any more questions?"

"Would you like some cheese?"

Harvey couldn't help liking the young man, within his reservation that the police had, no doubt, sent him precisely to be liked. Soften me up as much as you please, Harvey thought, but it doesn't help you; it only serves to release my own love, my nostalgia, for Effie. And he opened his mouth and spoke in praise of Effie, almost to his own surprise describing how she was merry at parties, explaining that she danced well and was fun to talk to. "She's an interesting woman, Effie."

"Intellectual?"

"We are all more intellectual than we know. She doesn't think of herself as an intellectual type. But under a certain stimulus, she is."

They were walking back to the commissariat. Harvey had half a mind to go home and let them come for him with an official summons, if they wanted. But it was only half a mind; the other half, mesmerized and now worked up about Effie, propelled him on to the police station with his companion.

"She tried some drugs, I suppose," said Pomfret.

"You shouldn't suppose so," said Harvey. "Effie is entirely anti-drug. It would be extraordinary if she's taken to drugs in the last two years."

"You must recognize," said Pomfret, "that she is lively and vital enough to be a member of a terrorist gang."

"Lively and vital," said Harvey, "lively and vital—one of those words is redundant."

Pomfret laughed.

"However," said Harvey, "it's out of the question that

she could be a terrorist." He had a suspicion that Pomfret was now genuinely fascinated by the images of Effie that Harvey was able to produce, Effie at a party, Effie an interesting talker, a rich man's wife; his imagination was involved, beyond his investigator's role, in the rich man's mechanism, his free intellectual will, his casual purchase of the château; Pomfret was fascinated by both Effie and Harvey.

"A terrorist," said Pomfret. "She obviously has an idealistic motive. Why did you leave her?"

The thought that Effie was a member of a terrorist band now excited Harvey sexually.

"Terrorist is out of the question," he said. "I left her because she seemed to want to go her own way. The marriage broke up, that's all. Marriages do."

"But on a hypothesis, how would you feel if you knew she was a terrorist?"

Harvey thought, I would feel I had failed her in action. Which I have. He said, "I can't imagine."

At the police station Pomfret left him in a waiting-room. Patiently sitting there was a lean-faced man with a dark skin gone to a muddy grey, bright small eyes and fine features. He seemed to be a Balkan. What was he doing there? It was after nine in the evening. Surely it was in the morning that he would come about his papers. Perhaps he had been picked up without papers? What sort of work was he doing in Epinal? He wore a black suit, shiny with wear; a very white shirt open at the neck; brown, very pointed shoes; and he had with him a brown cardboard brief-case with tinny locks, materials such as Harvey had only seen before in the form of a suitcase on a train in a remote part of Sicily. The object in Sicily had been old and battered, but his present companion's brief-case had a new-bought look. It was not the first time Harvey had noticed that poor people from Eastern Europe resembled, not only in their possessions and clothes, but in their build and expression, the poor of Western Europe years ago. Who he was, where he came from and why, Harvey was never to know, for he was just about to say something when the door opened and a policeman in uniform beckoned the man away. He followed with nervous alacrity and the door closed again on Harvey. Patience, pallor and deep anxiety: there goes suffering, Harvey reflected. And I found him interesting. Is it only by recognizing how flat would be the world without the sufferings of others that we know how desperately becalmed our own lives would be without suffering? Do I suffer on Effie's account? Yes, and perhaps I can live by that experience. We all need something to suffer about. But *Job*, my work on *Job*, all interrupted and neglected, probed into and interfered with: that is experience, too; real experience, not vicarious, as is often assumed. To study, to think, is to live and suffer painfully.

Did Effie really kill or help to kill the policeman in Paris whose wife was shopping in the suburbs at the time? Since he had left the police station on Saturday night he had recurrently put himself to imagine the scene. An interruption at a department store. The police arrive. Shots fired. Effie and her men friends fighting their way back to their waiting car (with Nathan at the wheel?). Effie, lithe and long-legged, a most desirable girl, and quick-witted, unmoved, aiming her gun with a good aim. She pulls the trigger and is away all in one moment. Yes, he could imagine Effie in the scene; she was capable of that, capable of anything.

"Will you come this way, please, Mr. Gotham?"

There was a stack of files on Chatelain's desk.

The rest of that night Harvey remembered as a sort of roll-call of his visitors over the past months; it seemed to him like the effect of an old-fashioned village policeman going his rounds, shining his torch on name-plates and door-knobs; one by one, each name surrounded by a nimbus of agitated suspicion as his friends' simple actions, their ordinary comings and goings came up for questioning. It was strange how guilty everything looked under the policeman's torch, how it sounded here in the police headquarters. Chatelain asked Harvey if he would object to the conversation being tape-recorded.

"No, it's a good thing. I was going to suggest it. Then you won't have to waste time asking me the same questions over and over again."

Chatelain smiled sadly. "We have to check." Then he selected one of the files and placed it before him.

"Edward Jansen," he said, "came to visit you."

"Yes, he's the husband of my wife's sister, Ruth, now separated. He came to see me last April."

Chatelain gave a weak smile and said, "Your neighbours seem to remember a suspicious-looking character who visited you last spring."

"Yes, I daresay that was Edward Jansen. He has red hair down to his shoulders. Or had. He's an actor and he's now famous. He is my brother-in-law through his marriage to my wife's sister, but he's now separated from his wife. A lot can happen in less than a year."

"He asked you why there were baby clothes on the line?"

"I don't remember if he actually asked, but he made

148

some remark about them because I answered, as you know, 'The police won't shoot if there's a baby in the house.' "

"Why did you say that?"

"I can't answer precisely. I didn't foresee any involvement with the police, or I wouldn't have said it."

"It was a joke?"

"That sort of thing."

"Do you still hear from Edward Jansen?" Chatelain opened one of the files.

"I haven't heard for some time."

Chatelain flicked through the file.

"There's a letter from him waiting for you at your house."

"Thanks. I expect you can tell me the contents."

"No, we can't."

"That could be taken in two senses," Harvey said.

"Well, you can take it in one sense: we haven't opened it. The name and address of the sender is on the outside of the envelope. As it happens, we know quite a lot about Mr. Jansen, and he doesn't interest us at the moment. He's also been questioned." Chatelain closed the file, evidently Edward's dossier; it was rather thin compared with some of the others. Chatelain took up another and opened it, as if starting on a new subject. Then, "What did you discuss with Edward Jansen last April?" he said.

"I can't recall. I know his wife, Ruth, was anxious for me to make a settlement on her sister and facilitate a divorce. I am sure we didn't discuss that very much, for I had no intention of co-operating with my wife to that end. I know we discussed the *Book of Job.*"

"And about Ruth Jansen. Did you invite her to stay?"

"No, she came unexpectedly with her sister's baby, about the end of August."

"Why did she do that?"

"August is a very boring month for everybody."

"You really must be serious, Mr. Gotham."

"It's as good a reason as any. I can't analyse the motives of a woman who probably can't analyse them herself."

Chatelain tapped the file. "She says here that she brought the baby, hoping to win you over to her view that the child would benefit if you made over a substantial sum of money to its mother, that is, to your wife Effie."

"If that's what Ruth says, I suppose it is so."

"She greatly resembles your wife."

"Yes, feature by feature. But of course, to anyone who knows them they are very different. Effie is more beautiful, really. Less practical than Ruth."

Pomfret came in and sat down. He was less free of manner in the presence of the other officer. He peered at the tape-recording machine as if to make sure everything was all right with it.

"So you had a relation with Mrs. Jansen."

"Yes."

"Your sister-in-law and wife of your friend."

"Yes, I grew fond of Ruth. I was particularly taken by the baby. Of course, by this time Ruth and Edward had parted."

"Things happen fast in your set."

"Well, I suppose the parting had been working up for a long time. Is there any point in all these questions?"

"Not much. We want to check, you see, against the statements made in England by the people concerned.

Did Ruth seem surprised when she heard that Effie was involved in the terrorist attacks?"

What were these statements of Ruth, of Edward, of others? Harvey said firmly, even as he felt his way, "She was very much afraid of the police, coming into our lives as they did. It was quite unforeseen. She could no more blame her sister for it than she could blame her for an earthquake. I feel the same, myself."

"She did not defend her sister?"

"She had no need to defend Effie to me. It isn't I who accuse Effie of being a terrorist. I say there is a mistake."

"Now, Nathan Fox," said the officer, reaching for a new file. "What do you know about him?"

"Not very much. He made himself useful to Ruth and Edward when they were living in London. He's a graduate but can't find a job. He came to my house, here, to visit Ruth and the baby for Christmas."

"He is a friend of your wife?"

"Well, he knows her, of course."

"He is a weak character?"

"No, in fact I think it shows a certain strength of character in him to have turned his hand to domestic work since he can't find anything else to do. He graduated at an English university, I have no idea which one."

"What about his friends. Girls or boys?"

"I know nothing about that."

"Why did he disappear from your house?"

"I don't know. He just left. Young people do."

"He had a telephone call and left overnight without saying good-bye."

"I believe so," said Harvey.

"He said the telephone call was from London. It wasn't."

"So I understand. I was working in my cottage that night. You must understand I'm very occupied, and all these questions of yours, and all these files, have nothing whatever to do with me. I've agreed to come here simply to help you to eliminate a suspect, my wife."

"But you have no idea why he should say he got a phone call from London, when he didn't. It must have been an internal call."

"Perhaps some girl of his turned up in France; maybe in Paris, and called him. And he skipped."

"Some girl or some boy?"

"Your question is beyond me. If I hear from him I'll ask him to get in touch with you. Perhaps he's come down with influenza."

Pomfret now spoke: "Why do you suggest that?" He was decidedly less friendly in French.

"Because people do come down with 'flu. They stay in bed. This time of year is rather the time for colds. Perhaps he's gone back to England to start a window-cleaning business. I believe I heard him speculating on the idea. There's always a need for window-cleaners."

"Anything else?" said Chatelain.

"The possibilities of Nathan Fox's whereabouts are such that I could go on all night and still not exhaust them."

"Would he go to join your wife if she asked him?"

Harvey considered. "That's also a possibility; one among millions."

"What are his political views?"

"I don't know. He never spoke of politics to me."

"Did he ask you for money?"

"After Christmas he asked me for his pay. I told him

that Ruth had the housekeeping money, and kept the accounts."

"Then Mrs. Jansen did give him money?"

"I only suppose," said Harvey, "that she paid him for his help. I really don't know."

"Do you think Ruth Jansen is a calculating woman? She left her husband, came to join you with the baby, induced you to buy the château—"

"She wanted the château because of a tree outside the house with a certain bird—how do you say 'wood-pecker'?"—Harvey put the word to Pomfret in English.

Pomfret didn't recognize the word.

"It makes a sound like a typewriter. It pecks at the wood of the tree."

"*Pic*," said Pomfret.

"Well, she liked the sound of it," said Harvey.

"Are you saying that is why you bought the château?"

"I'd already thought of buying it. And now, with Ruth and the baby, it was convenient to me."

"Ernest L. Howe," said Chatelain. "He came to see you, didn't he?"

"Yes, some time last autumn. He came to see his baby daughter. He wanted Ruth to go back to London with the baby and live with him. Which, in fact, she has now done. You see, he doesn't think of what's best for the child; he thinks of what's most pleasant for himself. To console his hurt pride that Effie walked out on him— and I don't blame her—he's persuaded her sister to go and live with him, using the child as an excuse. It's contemptible."

Harvey was aware that the two men were conscious of a change in his tone, that he was loosening up. Harvey didn't care. He had nothing, Effie had nothing, to lose by his expressing himself freely on the subject of Ernie Howe. He was tired of being what was so often called civilized about his wife's lover. He was tired of the questioning. He was tired, anyway, and wanted a night's sleep. He deliberately gave himself and his questioners the luxury of his true opinion of Ernie.

"Would you care for a drink?" said Pomfret.

"A double scotch," said Harvey, "with a glass of water on the side. I like to put in the water myself."

Chatelain said he would have the same. Pomfret disappeared to place the orders. Chatelain put a new tape in the recording machine while Harvey talked on about Ernie.

"He sounds like a shit," said Chatelain. "Let me tell you in confidence that even from his statement which I have in front of me here, he sounds like a shit. He stated categorically that he wasn't at all surprised that Effie was a terrorist, and further, he says that you know it."

"He's furious that Effie left him," Harvey said. "He thought she would get a huge alimony from me to keep him in comfort for the rest of his life. I'm sure she came to realize what he was up to, and that's why she left him."

Pomfret returned, followed by a policeman with a tray of drinks. It was quite a party. Harvey felt easier.

"I'm convinced of it," he said, and for the benefit of Pomfret repeated his last remarks.

"It's altogether in keeping with the character of the man, but he was useful," said Chatelain. He said to Pomfret, "I have revealed to M. Gotham what Ernest Howe stated about Effie Gotham."

And what Chatelain claimed Ernie had said was evidently true, for Pomfret quite spontaneously confirmed it: "Yes, I'm afraid he was hardly gallant about her. He is convinced she's a terrorist and that you know it."

"When did you get these statements?" said Harvey.

"Recently. Ernest Howe's came through from Scotland Yard on Sunday."

"You've got Scotland Yard to help you?"

"To a certain degree," said Chatelain, waving his right hand lightly, palm-upward.

Was he softening up these men, Harvey wondered, or they him?

"It would interest me," said Harvey, "to see the photograph of my wife that was taken of her by the police in Trieste, when she was arrested for shoplifting."

"You may see it, of course. But it isn't being handed out to the newspapers. It has been useful for close identification purposes by eye-witnesses. You will see it looks too rigid—like all police photos—to be shown to the public as the girl we are actually looking for. She is quite different in terrorist action, as they all are." He turned to Pomfret. "Can you find the Trieste photograph?"

Pomfret found it. The girl in the photo was looking straight ahead of her, head uplifted, eyes staring, against a plain light background. Her hair was darker than Effie's in real life, but that might be an effect of the flash-photography. It looked like Effie, under strain, rather frightened.

"It looks like a young shop-lifter who's been hauled in by the police," said Harvey.

"Do you mean to say it isn't your wife?" said Pomfret. "She gave her name as Signora Effie Gotham. Isn't it her?"

"I think it is my wife. I don't think it looks like the picture of a hardened killer."

155

"A lot can happen in a few months," said Chatelain. "A lot has happened to that young woman. Her battle-name isn't Effie Gotham, naturally. It is Marion."

In the meantime Pomfret had extracted from his papers the photograph of Effie that the police had found in Harvey's cottage. "You should have this back," said Pomfret. "It is yours."

"Thank you. You've made copies. I see this photo in every newspaper I open."

"It is the girl we are looking for. There is movement and life in that photograph."

"I think you should publish the police-photo from Trieste," said Harvey. "To be perfectly fair. They are both Effie. The public might not then be prejudiced."

"Oh, the public is not so subtle as to make these nice distinctions."

"Then why don't you publish the Trieste photograph?"

"It is the property of the Italian police. For them, the girl in their photograph is a kleptomaniac, and in need of treatment. They had put the treatment in hand, but she skipped off, as they all do."

"I thought she went to prison."

"She had a two weeks' sentence. That is a different thing from imprisonment. It was not her first offence, but she was no more than three days in prison. She agreed to treatment. She was supposed to register with the police every day, but of course—"

"Look," said Harvey. "My wife is suffering from an illness, kleptomania. She needs treatment. You are hounding her down as a terrorist, which she isn't. Effie couldn't kill anyone."

"Why did you leave her on the motorway in Italy?"

said Pomfret. "Was it because she stole a bar of chocolate? If so, why didn't you stand by her and see that she had treatment?"

"She has probably told Ernie Howe that story, and he has told you."

"Correct," said Chatelain.

"Well, if I'd given weight to a bar of chocolate, I would have stood by her. I didn't leave her over a bar of chocolate. To be precise, it was two bars."

"Why did you leave her?"

"Private reasons. Incompatibility, mounting up. A bar of chocolate isn't a dead policeman."

"We know," said Chatelain. "We know that only too well. We are not such fools as to confuse a shop-lifter with a dangerous assassin."

"But why," said Pomfret, "did you leave her? We think we know the answer. She isn't a kleptomaniac at all. Not at all. She stole, made the easy gesture, on ideological grounds. They call it proletarian re-appropriation. You must already have perceived the incipient terrorist in your wife; and on this silly occasion, suddenly, you couldn't take it. Things often happen that way."

"Let me tell you something," said Harvey. "If I'd thought she was a terrorist in the making, I would not have left her. I would have tried to reason her out of it. I know Effie well. She isn't a terrorist. She's a simple shop-lifter. Many rich girls are."

"Is she rich?"

"She was when she was with me."

"But afterwards?"

"Look, if she needed money, she could have sold her jewellery. But she hasn't. It's still in the bank. My lawyer told me."

"Didn't you say—I think you said—" said Pomfret, "that you only discussed the recent English translations of the Bible with your lawyer?"

"I said that was what we were discussing on Saturday morning, instead of listening to the news on the radio. I haven't said that I discussed nothing else with him. You see, I, too, am anxious to trace the whereabouts of my wife. She isn't your killer in Paris. She's somewhere else."

"Now, let us consider," said Chatelain, "her relations with Ernest Howe. He has stated that he knows her character. She is the very person, according to him, who would take up with a terrorist group. The Irish terrorists had her sympathy. She was writing a treatise on child-labour in England in the nineteenth century. She often—"

"Oh, I know all that," Harvey said. "The only difficulty is that none of her sympathies makes her a terrorist. She shares these sympathies with thousands of people, especially young people. The young are very generous. Effie is generous in spirit, I can say that."

"But she has been trying to get money out of you, a divorce settlement."

"That's understandable. I'm rich. But quite honestly, I hoped she'd come back. That's why I refused the money. She could have got it through the courts, but I thought she'd get tired of fighting for it."

"What do you mean, 'come back'?" said Pomfret. "It was you who left her."

"In cases of desertion in marriage, it is always difficult to say who is the deserter. There is a kind of constructional desertion, you know. Technically, yes, I left her. She also had left me. These things have to be understood."

"I understand," said Chatelain. "Yes, I understand your point."

Pomfret said, "But where is she getting the money from?"

"I suppose that the girl who calls herself Marion has funds from the terrorist supporters," said Harvey. "They are never short of funds. It has nothing whatsoever to do with my wife, Effie."

"Well, let us get back to your visitors, M. Gotham," said Chatelain. "Has there been anyone else besides those we have mentioned?"

"The police, and Anne-Marie."

"No-one else?"

"Clara," said Harvey. "Don't you want to hear about Clara?"

"Clara?"

"Clara is the niece of my wife's sister."

Chatelain was getting tired. He took a long moment to work out Harvey's representation, and was still puzzling while Pomfret was smiling. "The niece?" said Chatelain. "Whose daughter is she?"

"My wife's."

"You mean the infant?"

"That's right. Don't you have a dossier on Clara?" Harvey asked the security men.

"M. Gotham, this is serious. A man has been fatally shot. More deaths may follow. We are looking for a political fanatic, not a bar of chocolate. Can you not give us an idea, a single clue, as to where your wife can be hiding? It might help us to eliminate her from the enquiry."

"I wish I could find her, myself."

X

"I BROUGHT YOU some English mustard," said Auntie Pet. "They say English mustard in France is at a prohibitive price even compared to Canadian prices."

Harvey had slept badly after his late return from the session with the security police at Epinal. He hadn't shaved.

"You got home late," said Auntie Pet. Already, the château was her domain.

"I was with the police," said Harvey.

"What were you doing with them?" she said.

"Oh, talking and drinking."

"I shouldn't hob-nob too close with them," she said, "if I were you. Keep them in their place. I must say those plain-clothes officers who escorted me here were very polite. They were useful with the suitcases, too. But I kept them in their place."

"I should imagine you would," Harvey said.

They were having breakfast in the living room which the presence of Auntie Pet somehow caused to look very shabby. She was large-built, with a masculine, military face; grey eyes which generally conveyed a warning; heavy, black brows and a head of strong, wavy, grey hair. She was sewing a piece of stuff; some kind of embroidery.

"When I arrived," she said, "there was a crowd of reporters and photographers on the road outside the house. But the police soon got rid of them with their cars and motor-cycles. No problem." Her eyes rose from her sewing. "Harvey, you have let your house go into a state of dilapidation."

"I haven't had time to put it straight yet. Only moved in a few months ago. It takes time."

"I think it absurd that your maid brings her baby's washing to do in your house every day. Hasn't she got a house of her own? Why are you taking a glass of scotch with your breakfast?"

"I need it after spending half the night with the police."

"They were all right to me. I was glad of the ride. The prohibitive price of fares," said his aunt, as one multi-millionaire to another.

"I can well believe they were civil to you. I should hope they would be. Why shouldn't they be?" He looked at her solid, irreproachable shape, her admonishing face; she appeared to be quite sane; he wondered if indeed the police had been half-afraid of her. Anne-Marie was already tip-toeing around in a decidedly subdued way. Harvey added, "You haven't committed any of-fence."

"Have you?" she said.

"No."

"Well, I should have said you have. It's certainly an offence if you're going to attack the Bible in a foreign country."

"The French police don't care a damn about the Bible. It's Effie. One of their policemen has been shot, killed, and they think she's involved."

"Oh, no, not Effie," said Auntie Pet. "Effie is your wife. She is a Gotham as of now, unfortunately, what-ever she was before. No Gotham would stoop to harm a policeman. The police have always respected and looked up to us. And you're letting yourself go, Harvey. Just because your wife is not at home, there isn't any reason to neglect to shave."

Harvey escaped to go and shave, leaving Auntie Pet to quarrel with Anne-Marie, and walk about the grounds giving orders to the plain-clothes police, whom she took for gardeners and woodsmen, for the better upkeep of shrubs and flower-beds, for the cultivation of vegetables and the felling of over-shady trees. From his bathroom window Harvey saw her finding cigarette-ends on the gravel path, and chiding the men in full spate of Cana-dian French. Prompted by Anne-Marie, they took it fairly well; and it did actually seem to Harvey, as he found it did to Anne-Marie, that they were genuinely frightened of her, armed though they were to the full capacity of their leather jackets.

When Harvey came down he found in the living room a batch of press-cuttings which he at first presumed to be about himself and Effie; Stewart Cowper had left them behind. But a glance at the top of the bundle showed him Edward's face, now beardless. The cuttings were, in reality, all reviews of the play Edward had made such an amazing success in; they were apparently full of lavish praise of the new star, but Harvey put them aside for a more serene moment. Amongst some new mail, a letter from Edward was lying on the table. Edward's name and address was written on the back of the envelope. Maybe the police hadn't read it; maybe they had. Harvey left this aside, too, as Auntie Pet came back into the room.

"I have something to tell you," she said. "I have come all the way from Toronto to say it. I know it is going to hurt you considerably. After all, you are a Gotham, and must feel things of a personal nature, a question of your honour. But say it I had to. Not on the telephone. Not through the mail. But face to face. Your wife, Effie, is consorting with a young man in a commune, as they call it, in the mountains of California, east of Santa Barbara if I recall rightly. I saw her myself on the television in a documentary news-supplement about communes. They live by Nature and they have a sort of religion. They sleep in bags. They—"

"When did you see this?"

"Last week."

"Was it an old film—was it live?"

"I guess it was live. As I say, it was a news item, about a drug-investigation by the police, and they had taken this commune by surprise at dawn. The young people were all scrambling out of their bags and into their clothes. And I am truly sorry to tell you this, Harvey, but I hope you'll take it like a man: Effie was sleeping in a double bag, a double sleeping-bag, do you understand;

there was a young man right in there with her, and they got out of that bag sheer, stark naked."

"Are you sure it was Effie? Are you sure?"

"I remember her well from the time she came when you were engaged, and then from the wedding, and I have the wedding-photo of you both on my piano, right there in the sitting room where I go every day. I ought to recognize Effie when I see her. She was naked, with her hair hanging down her shoulders, and laughing, and then pulling her consort after her out of the extramarital bag, without shame; I am truly sorry, Harvey, to be the bearer of this news. To a Gotham. Better she killed a policeman. It's a question of honour. Mind you, I always suspected she was unvirtuous."

"You always suspected?"

"Yes, I did. All along I feared the worst."

"Are you sure," said Harvey, very carefully, "that perhaps your suspicions have not disposed you to imagine that the girl you saw on the television was Effie, when in fact it was someone who resembled her?"

"Effie is not like anybody else," said Auntie Pet.

"She resembles her sister," said Harvey.

"How could it be Ruth? Ruth is not missing, is she?"

"No. I don't say it could have been Ruth. I only say that there is one case where Effie looks like somebody else. I know of another."

"Who is that?"

"Job's wife, in a painting."

"Job's wife it could not be. She was a foolish woman but she never committed adultery in a sack. You should read your Bible, Harvey, before you presume to criticize it."

Harvey poured himself a drink.

"Don't get over-excited," said Auntie Pet. "I know this is a blow."

"Look, Auntie Pet, I must know the details, every detail. I have to know if you're absolutely sure, if you're right. Would you mind describing the man to me?"

"I hope you're not going to cite him as co-respondent, Harvey. You would have to re-play that news item in court. It would bring ridicule on our heads. You've had enough publicity."

"Just describe the young man she was with, please."

"Well, this seems like an interrogation. The young man looked like a Latin-Mediterranean type, maybe Spanish, young, thin. I didn't look closely, I was looking at Effie. She had nothing on."

Auntie Pet had not improved with the years. Harvey had never known her so awful. H thought, She is mistaken but at least, sincere. He said, "I must tell the police."

"Why?" said Auntie Pet.

"For many reasons. Not the least of which is that, if Effie and her friend are in California and decide to leave, they might come here, for instance, here to France, or here to see me; if they do that, they could be shot at sight."

"That's out of the question. Effie wouldn't dare come to your house, now. But if you tell the police how I saw them, the story will go round the world. And the television picture, too. Think of your name."

Harvey got through to the commissariat. "My wife has been seen in California within the last few days."

"Who saw her?"

"My aunt."

"Ah, the aunt," said the police inspector.

"She says she saw her in a youth-documentary on the television."

"We had better come and talk to your aunt."

"It isn't necessary."

"Do you believe your aunt?"

"She's truthful. But she might be mistaken. That's all I have to say."

"I would like to have a word with her."

"All right," said Harvey. "You'll find her alone because I'm going down to my cottage to work."

He then rang Stewart Cowper in London but found he was out of the office. "Tell him," said Harvey to the secretary, "that I might want him to go to the United States for me."

He had been in his cottage half-an-hour when he saw the police car going up the drive, with the two security men from Paris. He wished them well of Auntie Pet.

Harvey had brought his mail with him, including Edward's letter.

In his old environment, almost smiling to himself with relief at being alone again, sat for a while sorting out his thoughts.

Effie and Nathan in a commune in California: it was quite likely. Effie and Nathan in Paris, part of a band of killers: not unlikely.

He began to feel uneasy about Auntie Pet, up there at the house, being questioned by the security men. He was just getting ready to go and join them, and give his aunt a show of support, when the police car with the two men inside returned, passed his cottage, and made off. Either they had made short work of Auntie Pet or she of them. Harvey suspected the latter. Auntie Pet had been separated from Uncle Joe for as long as Harvey could remember. They lived in separate houses. There was no question of a divorce, no third parties, no lovers and mistresses. "I had to make a separate arrangement," Uncle Joe had once confided to Harvey. "She would have made short work of me if I'd stayed."

Harvey himself had never felt in danger of being made short work of by his aunt. Probably there was something in his nature, a self-sufficiency, that matched her own.

He wondered how much to believe of what she had told him. He began to wonder such things as why a news supplement from California should be shown on a main network in Toronto. Auntie Pet wasn't likely to tune in to anything but a main network. He wondered why she had felt it necessary to come to France to give him these details; and at the same time he knew that it was quite reasonable that she should do so. It would certainly be, for her, a frightful tale to tell a husband and a Gotham.

And to his own amazement, Harvey found himself half-hoping she was wrong. Only half-hoping; but still, the thought was there: he would rather think of Effie as a terrorist than laughing with Nathan, naked, in a mountain commune in California. But really, thought Harvey, I don't wish it so. In fact, I wish she wasn't a terrorist; and in fact, I think she is. Pomfret was right; I saw the terrorist in Effie long ago. Even if she isn't the killer they're looking for, but the girl in California, I won't live with her again.

He decided to get hold of Stewart Cowper later in the day, when he was expected back at his office. Stewart would go to California and arrange to see a re-play of the programme Auntie Pet had seen. Stewart would find out if Effie was there. Or he would go himself; that would be the decent thing to do. But he knew he wouldn't go himself. He was waiting here for news of Effie. He was writing his monograph on the *Book of Job* as he had set himself to do. ("Live?—Our servants can do it for us.") He wouldn't even fight with Ernie Howe himself; if necessary, Stewart would do it for him.

He opened Edward's letter.

Dear Harvey,

The crocs at the zoo have rather lacklustre eyes, as can be expected. Perhaps in their native habitat their eyes are "like the eyelids of the dawn" as we find in *Job*, especially when they're gleefully devouring their prey. Yes, their eyelids are vertical. Perhaps leviathan is not the crocodile. The zoo bores me to a degree.

I wish you could come over and see the play before it closes. My life has changed, of course. I don't feel that my acting in this play, which has brought me so much success, is really any different from my previous performances in films, plays, t.v. I think the psychic forces, the influences around me have changed. Ruth wasn't good for me. She made me into a sort of desert. And now I'm fertile. (We are the best of friends, still. I saw her the other day. I don't think she's happy with Ernie Howe. She's only sticking to him because of Clara, and as you know she's pregnant herself at long last. She claims, and of course I believe her, that she's preg by you. —Congratulations.) Looking back—and it seems a

long time to look back although it's not even a year
—I feel my past life had a drabness that I wasn't
fully aware of at the time. It lies like a shabby old
pair of trousers that I've let fall on the bedroom
floor: I'll never want to wear *those* again. It isn't
only the success and the money, although I don't
overlook that aspect of things—I don't want to
crow about them, esp to you. It's simply a new sense
of possibility. One thing I do know is when I'm
playing a part and when I'm not. I used to "play a
part" most of the time. Now I only do it when I'm
onstage. You should come over and see the play.
But I suspect that possibly you can't. The police
quizzed me and I made a statement. What could I
say? Very little. Fortunately the public is sympathetic towards my position—brother-in-law, vir-
tually *ex*-brother-in-law of a terrorist. (Our divorce
is going through.) It isn't a close tie.

I've almost rung you up on several occasions. But
then I supposed your phone was bugged, and felt it
better not to get involved. Reading the papers—of
course you can't trust them—it seems you're standing by Effie, denying that she's the wanted girl, and
so on. Now, comes this ghastly murder of the policeman. I admire your stance, but do you feel it
morally necessary to protect her? I must say, I find
it odd that having left her as you did, you now refuse
to see (or admit?) how she developed. To me (and
Ruth agrees with me) she has always had this criminal streak in her. I know she is a beautiful girl, but
there are plenty of lovely girls like Effie. You can't
have been so desperately in love with her. Quite
honestly, when you were together, I never thought

you were really crazy about her. I don't like giving advice, but you should realize that something tragic has happened to Effie. She is a fanatic—she always had that violent, reckless streak. There is nothing, Harvey, nothing at all that anyone can do for her. You shouldn't try. Conclude your work on *Job*, then get away and start a new life. If your new château is as romantic and grand as Ruth says it is, I'd love to see it. I'll come, if you're still there, when the play closes. It'll be good to see you.

Affectionately,
Edward

Harvey's reply:

Dear Edward,

That was good of you to go to the zoo for me. You say the zoo bores you to a degree. What degree?

I congratulate you on your success. It was always in you, so I'm not surprised. No, I can't leave here at present. Ruth would be here still if it were not that the place is bristling with the police—no place for Clara whom I miss terribly.

As to your advice, do you remember how Prometheus says, "It's easy for the one who keeps his foot on the outside of suffering to counsel and preach to the one who's inside"? I will just say that I'm not taking up Effie's defence. I hold that there's no proof that the girl whom the police are looking for is Effie. A few people have "identified" her from a photograph.

Auntie Pet has arrived from Toronto wearing those remarkable clothes that so curiously belie her puritanical principles. This morning she was wearing what appeared to be the wallpaper. Incidentally, she recognized Effie in a recent television documentary about a police-raid on a mountain commune in California. She was with a man whose description could fit Nathan Fox.

I've been interrogated several times. What they can't make out is why I'm here in France, isolated, studying *Job*. The last time it went something like this:

Interrogator—You say you're interested in the problem of suffering?

Myself—Yes.

Interrogator—Are you interested in violence?

Myself—Yes, oh, yes. A fascinating subject.

Interrogator—*Fascinating?*

Almost anything you answer is suspect. At the same time, supermarkets have been bombed, banks robbed, people terrorized and a policeman killed. They are naturally on edge.

There is a warrant of arrest out for my wife. The girl in the gang, whoever she is, could be killed.

But "no-one pities men who cling wilfully to their sufferings" (*Philoctetes*—speech of Neoptolemus). I'm not even sure that I suffer, I only endure distress. But why should I analyse myself? I am analysing the God of *Job*.

I hope the mystery of Effie can be cleared up and when your show's over you can come and see *Château Gotham*. Ruth will undoubtedly come.

I'm analysing the God of *Job*, as I say. We are back to the Inscrutable. If the answers are valid then it is the questions that are all cock-eyed.

> *Job* 38: 2–3: Who is this that darkeneth counsel by words without knowledge?
>
> Gird up now thy loins like a man; for I will demand of thee, and answer thou me.

It is God who asks the questions in Job's book.

Now I hope you'll tell Ruth she can come here with Clara when the trouble's over, and have her baby. I'm quite willing to take on your old trousers, Edward, and you know I wish you well in your new pair, your new life.

Yours,
Harvey

PART III

XI

"So the lord blessed the latter end of Job more than his beginning." It was five days since Stewart Cowper had left for California. He had telephoned once, to say he had difficulty in getting the feature identified which Auntie Pet had seen, but he felt he was on the track of it now. There definitely had been a news item of that nature.

"Ring me as soon as you know," said Harvey.

Meantime, since he was near the end of his monograph on *Job*, he finished it. The essay had taken him over three years to complete. He was sad to see his duty all ended, his notes in the little room of the cottage now neatly stacked, and his manuscript, all checked and revised, ready to be photocopied and mailed to the typist in London (Stewart Cowper's pretty secretary).

The work was finished and the Lord had blessed the

latter end of Job with precisely double the number of sheep, camels, oxen and she-asses that he had started out with. Job now had seven sons and three daughters, as before. The daughters were the most beautiful in the land. They were called Jemima, Kezia and Keren-happuch, which means Box of Eye-Paint. Job lived another hundred and forty years. And Harvey wondered again if in real life Job would be satisfied with this plump reward, and doubted it. His tragedy was that of the happy ending.

He took his manuscript to St. Dié, had it photocopied and sent one copy off to London to be typed. He was anxious to get back to the château in case Stewart should ring with news. He hadn't told Auntie Pet of Stewart's mission, but somehow she had found out, as was her way, and had mildly lamented that her story should be questioned.

"You're just like the police," she said. "They didn't actually say they didn't believe me, but I could see they didn't."

He got back to the château just in time to hear the telephone. It was from the police at Epinal.

"You have no doubt heard the news, M. Gotham."

"No. What now?"

"The FLE gang were surrounded and surprised an hour ago in an apartment in Paris. They opened fire on our men. I regret to say your wife has been killed. You will come to Paris to identify the body."

"I think my wife is in California."

"We take into account your state of mind, Monsieur, but we should be obliged if—"

Anne-Marie was standing in the doorway with her head buried in her hands.

L'Institut Médico-Légal in Paris. Her head was bound up, turban-wise, so that she looked more than ever like Job's wife. Her mouth was drawn slightly to the side.

"You recognize your wife, Effie Gotham?"

"Yes, but this isn't my wife. Where is she? Bring me my wife's body."

"M. Gotham, you are overwrought. It displeases us all very much. You must know that this is your wife."

"Yes, it's my wife, Effie."

"She opened fire. One of our men was wounded."

"The boy?"

"Nathan Fox. We have him. He was caught while trying to escape."

Harvey felt suddenly relieved at the thought that Nathan wasn't in California with Effie.

The telephone rang when, finally, he got back to the château. It was from Stewart. "I've seen a re-play of the feature, Harvey," he said. "It looks like Effie but it isn't."

"I know," said Harvey.

He said to Auntie Pet, "Did you really think it was Effie in that mountain commune? How could you have thought so?"

"I did think so," said Auntie Pet. "And I still think so. That's the sort of person Effie is."

Anne-Marie said, "I'll be saying good-bye, now."

XII

EDWARD DRIVES ALONG the road between Nancy and St. Dié. It is the end of April. All along the way the cherry trees are in flower. He comes to the grass track that he took last year. But this time he passes by the cottage, bleak in its little wilderness, and takes the wider path through a better-tended border of foliage, to the château.

Ruth is there, already showing her pregnancy. Clara staggers around her play-pen. Auntie Pet, wrapped in orange and mauve woollens, sits upright on the edge of the sofa, which forms a background of bright yellow and green English fabrics for her. Harvey is there, too.

"You've cut your hair," says Harvey.

"I had to," says Edward, "for the part."

It is later, when Clara has gone to bed, that Edward gives Harvey a message he has brought from Ernie Howe.

"He says if you want to adopt Clara, you can. He doesn't want the daughter of a terrorist."

"How much does he want for the deal?"

"Nothing. That amazed me."

"It doesn't amaze me. He's a swine. Better he wanted money than for the reason he gives."

"I quite agree," says Edward. "What will you do now that you've finished *Job?*"

"Live another hundred and forty years. I'll have three daughters, Clara, Jemima and Eye-Paint."